Anonymous

Fables Calculated for the Amusement and Instruction of Youth

Originally Dedicated to a young prince...

Anonymous

Fables Calculated for the Amusement and Instruction of Youth
Originally Dedicated to a young prince...

ISBN/EAN: 9783744767620

Printed in Europe, USA, Canada, Australia, Japan

Cover: Foto ©Andreas Hilbeck / pixelio.de

More available books at **www.hansebooks.com**

F A B L E S

CALCULATED FOR THE

Amusement and Instruction of

Y O U · T H;

Originally dedicated to

A Y O U N G P R I N C E,

For whofe Improvement they were written.

TAKEN FROM THE FRENCH.

———————————Let mortals learn,
When in obedience to the Gods they tread
The doubtful paths of deftiny, to affront
The dreadful'ft dangers with undaunted fpirit;—
Let them not, even in worft extremes, defpair;
For while they keep to virtue's narrow paths,
With guards invincible they march furrounded :
The Gods who furely guide them on their way,
From them no more than from themfelves can ftray,
For virtue's of divinity a ray !

T A U N T O N:

Printed and Sold for the Translator,
By J. POOLE:
Sold alfo by Scatcherd and Whitaker, Ave-Maria Lane, and
R. V. Brooke, Cheapfide, London ; A. Small, Trowbridge;
M. Luckman, Coventry, and by other Booksellers.

M DCC LXXXIX.

P R E F A C E.

THESE valuable FABLES were firſt printed by a Bookſeller, who, devoid of all Ambition, centered every wiſh within the bounds of mediocrity, and contented with acquiring, by his Trade, a competency, neglected to exert thoſe ſanguine endeavors in extending ·that unlimited circulation of them, to which their merit ſo juſtly entitled them : it may therefore be ſaid, with great propriety, that they are preſented to the Public, as a new Work, well deſerving the attention of all thoſe any way intereſted in the Education of Youth, and particularly ſo of Parents, whoſe tenderneſs would render them deſirous of conveying Inſtruction in the moſt pleaſing manner.

A2   Fables

Fables poffefs this advantage over every other work of a light kind, that they are always new; —always entertaining to the young, and always approved of by the old, as the eafieft and moft agreeable channel through which they can, without appearing in the forbidding character of a Cenfor, correct many Faults, and fow the feeds of every Virtue, at the earlieft period of life; a period when the Judgment is too weak to bear a ftronger cultivation, or to feel the more forcible incitements to Virtue.

The

The Editor's

ADVERTISEMENT.

IF the Roman Laws decreed an Oaken Crown to thofe who fhould be fortunate enough to fave the Life of a Citizen, furely fome regard is due to thofe Bookfellers, who, in reviving the Writings of Authors whofe Works tend to the improvement of the Mind, and to the correcting the Errors of the Heart, perform a public Service. Next to faving a Life, fhould be efteemed the rendering that life an Ornament to Society.

In thefe Fables Youth will not only find the ftrongeft Incitements to Virtue, but the foundeft Maxims of political Wifdom; and at the fame time that they inculcate thefe, they fupport, by Example, the ftricteft adherence to the dictates of Religion.

They will warn Young Minds againft the Artifice, Cruelty, and Ingratitude to which the depravity of Human Nature is fubject. The Reader will alfo find, in moft Inftances,

that

that the Punifhment clofely follows the Crime; where it does not,—where they fee the Inno-cent fall Victims to Villainy, (which is fometimes permitted, no doubt, for wife purpofes) it will, by interefting their Feelings in favor of the un-protected, make them more fenfibly feel, and confequently, more warmly cultivate the love of Juftice, and render them acquainted with the Human Mind; a melancholy, but neceffa-ry Knowledge, which it has been the endeavor of the Author to render as agreeable as poffi-ble; cloathing Advice and Inftruction under the fafcinating appearance of Fiction, that it may fteal on the Mind with the infinuating mildnefs of Friendfhip, inftead of enforcing itfelf with the feverity of Wifdom

The ardent Wifh of becoming ferviceable to my fellow-creatures, enabled me to overcome the very great Difficulty which attended the reviving a Work fo very obfolete, both from its great Age, and the roughnefs and vulgarity which prevailed in Publications of the barba-rous period at which it was written; and the many Errors in the language, which has fince been fo much improved, and fo greatly refined: But where I could, with any propriety, leave Expreffions, whofe originality and force I fear-ed to leffen by correction, I have done it, though entirely contrary to the Style I fhould myfelf adopt.

It

It was unneceſſary to make any further alteration than what would render it unexception-
able to the generality of the world ; and in
many parts there was no other employment for
my pen than to give a more eaſy flow of Words
to the ſame Senſe, which the change of Style
in the preſent Age had rendered ſtiff and ob-
ſcure. I by no means claim any Merit, but
what the well-judging will deem me deſerving
of, for reſcuing from oblivion, Fables ſo calculated for Youth, by blending Inſtruction
with Amuſement.

The

The Translator's

ADVERTISEMENT.

THE Motives which induced the Editor to undertake the arduous Tafk of reviving fo old a Work, (almoft configned to oblivion) aĉuated the Tranflator to attempt the lefs difficult one, of prefenting it in Englifh, for the Amufement of Children, too young to have acquired a fufficient Knowledge of the French to profit by fo excellent a Work ; and to extend its Ufefulnefs, by rendering it intelligible to thofe who are not to be inftructed in the French Language.

Thefe Fables were printed in *One Thoufand, fix Hundred, and fifty nine,* and from their Antiquity, claim the Merit of all their Beauties being Original.

F A B.

T H E

C O N T E N T S.

F A B L E S.

FABLE I.

The SHEPHERD, WOLF, and FOX.

Great humility in an enemy is always suspicious.

A SHEPHERD was very much surprised, one day, to see a certain animal

B   mal

mal, which, on account of its diftance, he could not perfectly diftinguifh, dance to the found of his bagpipe. Some days afterwards it again appeared in the fame dancing humour, but had fcarcely continued this exercife half an hour, when the Shepherd faw, advancing towards him, a Fox, who gaily accofted him, faying; "that he had fome news to acquaint him with, for which he hardly expected credit". The Shepherd lending an attentive ear, the Fox thus began:

"The Wolf moft ardently wifhes he could appeafe, with his blood, the hatred which has fo long fubfifted betwixt his race and thofe of your flock: His juftice leads him to condemn the inveteracy of his relations, which blinds them to the good qualities of your fheep, and which has deftroyed that charming, that focial intercourfe he is too fenfible of not to efteem as highly valuable—as an acquifition the moft defirable, with animals famed for their virtue, mildnefs, and humanity—animals who are the very emblem of friendfhip itfelf: Added to the above confiderations, the irrefiftible, the fafcinating power your bagpipe acquires from your unequalled fkill and judgment, (that, even at this diftance, the harmony is fo exquifite he cannot refrain from dancing

to

to its heavenly founds)—he is induced to requeft, by me, the honor of paying his refpects to you, and reconciling all ancient feuds and animofities; living in future, in a mutual interchange of kindneffes and civilities:—I'll pawn my honor" continued the Fox, " you will thank me, fome time hence, for bringing about a reconciliation which will fecure to you an amiable and agreeable acquaintance; and above all, a fincere friend",

"Though I have well-founded reafons for fufpecting one who employs fuch an ambaffador," replied the Shepherd, (who had long known there was a ftrict league formed between them) " yet I by no means object to the overtures which the Wolf has condefcended to make me: He is perfectly welcome to vifit my fheep; to converfe with them freely, and to dance undifturbed to the found of my bagpipe, which will both do me honor, and give me pleafure; provided he will confent to come unarmed, proving his inclination to peace and a final ceffation of hoftilities, by leaving his teeth and his nails behind him, which are by no means requifite in converfation, or neceffary in dancing".

The

The Fox finding that all the art and flattery he had exerted, to feduce the Shepherd into a reliance on his profeffions, had only confirmed him in the fufpicions he had entertained of his treaçhery, retired with precipitation.

M O R A L.

By the meffenger you may generally judge of the good or bad intention of his employer.

FAB.

II. The PRINCE and The SILK-WORMS.

We too often fly from many things as in-convenient and disagreeable, which, upon re-flection, we should find of the utmost utility.

A Young Prince, seeking shelter from the heat of the day in a valley plant-ed with mulberry trees, found himself ex-tremely incommoded by the path being en-tirely covered with the cods of Silk-worms, which lying in the form of eggs, prevented his walking with ease, from an apprehensi-on of breaking them: The wind at the same time blowing some of the floss from the cods, against his face, became at last

B3   so

fo troublefome as to deprive him of the
pleafure and refrefhment he had promifed
himfelf in his walk; and his patience being
exhaufted, he at laft gave way to his pee-
vifhnefs, and with unmanly anger, kicked
fome with violence from the path, while
others he crufhed beneath his feet; when
his attention was arrefted by a found iffu-
ing out of one of the cods, and he diftinctly
heard thefe words.

" Wherefore ufe, thus cruelly, thofe without whom you would be in want of that
cloak which now decorates your fhoulders,
—without whom there would ceafe to be
any diftinction between you and the mean-
eft of your fubjects, who are coarfely cloath-
ed in woollen. Know, Prince, that to the
defpicable infect, whom in your impatience
you have annihilated with contempt, you
are indebted, not only for the gaudy deco-
ration of your perfon, but for fome of the
principal articles in that commerce which
brings riches into your kingdom:—Silks,
fattins, velvets, damafks and taffities would
not grace your manufactories, or fupport
your dignity and rank, unlefs we exifted to
fupply the filk.

Convinced

Convinced by this addrefs, of the imprudence, as well as cruelty of his behaviour,
this Prince by no means thought it a degradation to fhew he repented of it as a folly,
and regretted it as an unamiable licenfe of
temper, by his generous offer of having a
place built on purpofe near his own palace,
where they might with more convenience
fpin their filk.

"We will obey you," anfwered a Butterfly, " but at the fame time will fearleflly
acknowledge (for we have not been bred at
courts) that great as thou art, as a man and
as a Prince, thou doft not poffefs the power of rendering us any fervice but that of
leaving us to nature; who after having
made us flaves upon earth, to perform that
duty for which we were created, releafes us
from drudgery, by transforming us from
catterpillers into Butterflies; giving us
wings, and permitting us to feek our food
and pleafure in another element".

M O R A L.

When reafon blames you, never let obftinacy make you perfevere in filencing her dictates.

III. The GARDENER and DOG.

*The defigning will pretend to an averfion
they do not feel, to throw you off your guard,
where they intend to deceive you.*

A Young Woman who had lately become a Widow, and whofe whole
fubfiftence entirely depended upon the pro-
duce of her garden, was one day, when bufinefs made it neceffary for her to leave it in
truft, greatly diftreffed in whom fhe fhould
place that confidence.

Among thofe on whofe gratitude fhe had
a claim, from the care and attention they
had

had experienced from her, were a Fox, a Monkey, a Hog, and a Goat; each of whom thought himself moft deferving of the diftinction, and each officioufly offered as the propereft protector of her garden during her abfence; alledging thofe reafons they thought moft convincing, and vouching as proofs, what appeared to them to fpeak moft forcibly in favor of their honefty and gratitude.

The Monkey firft addreffed the Gardener. "Why feel diftruft in me, whofe worft enemy can only charge me with being roguifh from an innocent vivacity, which fometimes may lead me into a little mifchief that cannot materially injure any one, and has often been forgiven by you in confideration of the mirth it has created; but this fhould not impeach my honefty:—Depend therefore upon me, who have, befides, no inducement to pilfer you; fince a few nuts or a fmall apple comprifes all my wants and bounds all my wifhes".

The Hog urged his claim on his want of tafte, which led him to efteem that fruit as the moft delicious which lies rotted and neglected under the trees, and which it would be doing a fervice to remove.

The

The pretenfions of the Fox were founded on his known want of fkill and agility in climbing, and his natural integrity; but what would be, if poffible, to him, a more forcible incitement to honefty, was the very great refpect he felt towards fo amiable and charming a miftrefs, and the high fenfe he had of that goodnefs fhe had fo often condefcended to extend to him; thefe were ties which bound him with an irrefiftible force, that abfolutely compelled him to exert the moft ardent endeavors in ftrictly performing his duty; and which, on trial, would prove him the moft faithful of her fervants; an affertion he did not make through vanity, but from his confcience telling him it was a panegyric, juftice herfelf, in her fevereft humour, would decree him as moft truly his due.

"For my part," faid the Goat, "I have ever lived irreproachably, without either giving offence, or doing an injury to any one; added to that, nature, and cuftom, (half-fifter to the former) prove me perfectly difinterefted in offers of fervice, for no kind of fruit, let it be ripe or green, fweet or bitter, is ever allowed to form a part of my diet, which is confined to an handful of fimple herbs, or a lock of hay and a little

grafs

grafs; therefore you may fafely banifh all
fears that felfifh motives might bribe me to
forfeit your confidence.

"I return you all, my thanks for your
feveral offers of affiftance," replied the Widow; "but all your arguments and reafons,
though each differing from the other, have
failed in convincing me that either of you
are entitled to claim the diftinction you
make pretenfions to, or that you poffefs
thofe qualities that fhould in themfelves
bear teftimony of the confidence you deferve to have placed in you".

"The Fox, for inftance, poffeffes fo
much cunning fenfe, fhrewd artifice, and
malicious craft, that would render it dangerous he fhould be trufted by a fimple
country woman, who is particularly open
to deceit from her ignorance of the world
and her depending upon the fincerity and
goodnefs of her heart as the guide of her
conduct".

"The Monkey is too expenfive a guard;
for not contented with being mifchievoufly
extravagant, in wantonly wafting the fruit,
and deftroying more than he eats, he car-
ries a bag under his chin which he keeps
conftantly

constantly filled with whatever comes in his way ; of which, to do him justice, he is more a spendthrift than a glutton, but not less detrimental to my interest.

"The Goat, it is true, does not eat fruit, but causes me a more irreparable injury in the destruction of my trees, by depriving them of their bark, and thereby killing them :—

" And as for the Hog, the making choice of him would entail absolute ruin on me;— to his gluttony he would sacrifice my fruit, and devour my vegetables ;—with his uncouth snout, root up more trees in a day than he would find planted in an acre of ground—and entirely demolish my garden in turning up the earth to seek under it for roots to satisfy his gormandizing appetite.

" Therefore, the most judicious decision I can form, is to decline your various offers, and to determine in favor of the Dog, who equally as averse to the rind of trees as to all the other productions of a garden, can have no inducement to injure me, where no advantage can accrue to himself: His general character, for faithfulness of heart and intrepidity of spirit, confirms my hopes that

that I may, without fear of repenting, depend upon his fidelity—truſt with ſafety on his ſagacity and vigilance for removing from my ſituation all thoſe who have any ſuſpicious appearance of evil intentions—and that I may implicitly rely on his undaunted courage in defending it, whilſt he has life, againſt the moſt vigorous attack of the enemies of induſtry and honeſty.

M O R A L.

The placing a blind confidence in domeſtics and dependents, argues a weak underſtanding, and is generally puniſhed with infolence, ingratitude, a perfeᐸt confuſion in your affairs, and very frequently, the total ruin of your fortune.

FAB.

IV. The PANTHER and the LION.

Ambition in an envious, turbulent mind,
is the nurfe of fedition and rebellion; and
when united with power, the fafety of the ftate
requires its immediate extinction.

A PANTHER, who had looked forward with very fanguine hopes and
pretenfions of retaining the peaceable pof-
feffion of a very confiderable foreft, the
government of which he had for a long
time ufurped, finding the Lion had prefented it to the elephant, and that he was expected to offer his immediate refignation,
with all the refpect and duty of loyalty;
unable

unable to bear the difappointment of long-indulged expectations, broke out into the moſt difr⬛⬛⬛ ⬛nd injurious expreſſions againſt ⬛⬛⬛⬛⬛, and the moſt violent threats ⬛⬛⬛⬛ng himſelf (with the indi⬛ crimi⬛ ⬛f narrow ſouls) on the new gov⬛⬛⬛; ſwearing he would lie in ambuſh for ⬛⬛⬛, and ſacrifice him to his loſt hopes; then working himſelf up to that pitch of frenzy, which makes impoſſibilities appear eaſy to be executed, he, with the raſh pre-. ſumption of madneſs, vowed nought ſhould appeaſe his anger, till he had extirpated every animal at variance with him in the foreſt, and laid it waſte by the deſtruction of all its trees.

This violence was not confined to words alone, his deſtructive actions fully proved him ſerious in his determined cruelty, and having formed a league with ſome audaci-ous rebels, he was ſoon ſtrong enough to give chaſe to thoſe he had devoted as vic-tims to his diſappointed ambition; which he did, with ſuch ſucceſsful fury, that it was found neceſſary, as the only means of ſecu-ring the perſon of the Lion, to lay a trap for him; which being immediately execut-ed, with a ſkill his ungoverned rage prevent-ed him from being aware of, he, with ſeveral others,

others, became prifoners. His friends (like all friends in guilt) finding themf⬛⬛ thus unexpectedly detected, fought th⬛⬛⬛lon by meanly turning evidence again⬛⬛⬛ ther; and attributing their apparen⬛⬛ on to the cruelty and tyranny he had ex⬛⬛⬛ force them to a rebellion much aga⬛⬛ir inclination and which they moft fo⬛ re- pented of, recommended themfelves to that mercy they would have proved them- felves deferving of, could they have acted from the loyalty of their own hearts.

The accufation of the Panther's temerity and fevere exercife of affumed authority, being corroborated by all the other animals, the Lion refolved to give his free pardon to the accomplices of the Panther, referv- ing for him the fevereft and moft exempla- ry punifhment; which in the heat of his an- ger, he was determined to fee executed himfelf.

He had already arrived at the place of execution above half an hour, burning with the moft ardent defire of vengeance, and impatiently expecting the moment when he could fully gratify it:—At laft he faw the culprit advancing towards him with a ftep fo flow and grave, accompanied with
                                             fuch

fuch a confcious hopelefs melancholy, it
▮▮▮▮▮▮ his generous heart, as
▮▮▮▮▮▮er; but when he be-
▮▮▮▮▮▮y of his fpotted fkin,
▮▮▮▮▮▮nge was extinguifhed
w▮▮▮▮▮▮reaft, and riveting his
e▮▮▮▮▮▮preffive of the higheft
a▮▮▮▮▮▮dulged them in the plea-
fu▮▮▮▮▮▮ding one of nature's moft ex-
q▮▮▮▮e works, till he was unable to contain himfelf any longer:—

"Never, never fhall it be faid," cried he,
"I fentenced to death, an animal whofe
beauty is fuch an ornament to my foreft;
or that I wanted clemency towards one
who poffeffes fuch great qualities and fuch
rare endowments, as may, when he be-
comes fenfible of his fault, render him one
of the moft valuable of my fubjects. Re-
leafe him! and may he be grateful for the
life I give him; but let him carry that
chain fufpended about his neck, that I may
have it in my power to take him with eafe,
fhould he ever be guilty of the fame crime
again".

C   MORAL-

M O R A L.

Great abilities frequently 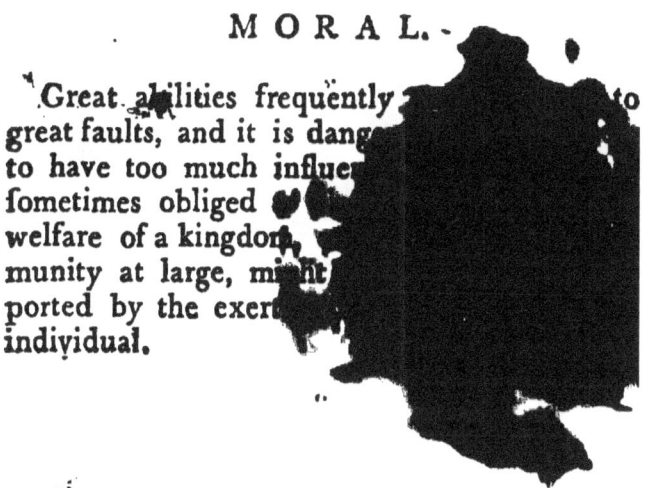 to great faults, and it is dang to have too much influe sometimes obliged welfare of a kingdo munity at large, m ported by the exer individual.

V.

V. The GENTLEMAN and MONKEY.

*Buffoonry, very frequently, gains more inte-
reſt in the hearts of the great, than wiſdom.*

FABLE.

A GENTLEMAN, who had amuſed
himſelf for ſome time with the ridiculous tricks of a Greyhound Puppy,
baniſhed him on his committing the
mighty crime of deſtroying, in one of his
pranks, a pair of ſilk ſtockings. A Paro-
quet was next promoted to the honor of
favorite, but ceaſing to talk, from ſome
complaint that attacked her, ſhe was like-
wiſe diſcarded, and a Monkey ſucceeded
her in her Maſter's heart; and as his only

C2   virtue

virtue was mifchievoufnefs, there was every
probability of his keeping in favor long
as ever he could fawn, play,
others, without including
" Do whatever you thin
he to him one day that he h
larly entertained him, "you have
berty from me to follow your inc
in every thing, and to indulge your mirth,
as whim fhall direct ".

This licence the Monkey underſtood in
the full extent of the words, and he firſt
availed himfelf of this permiſſion by pinch-
ing the footman, fcratching the pages, and
throwing down the attendants, by flily
creeping between their legs, while attentive to their bufinefs; the wit of which
appeared to his Maſter fo poignantly di-
verting, that he daily increaſed in favor;
which rendering him more boldly familiar,
he requeſted to be permitted to fit at din-
ner on the corner of the table, which was
immediately granted, with the additional
indulgence of eating off his fond Maſter's
plate. Perceiving the influence he had
gained, and that all his tricks highly delighted and entertained his Patron, he
thought he might gratify his inclination to
drefs his hair, which he was immediately

ly allowed, with many applaufes for in-
venting-▓ ▓▓▓▓ fo calculated to create mirth
▓▓d ▓▓▓▓▓▓

▓ ▓▓▓▓▓▓▓▓▓▓▓▓▓ perfuaded that his liberty
w▓▓▓▓▓▓▓▓▓ and that the more capri-
cio▓▓▓▓ ridiculous he was, the more he
rai▓▓▓▓▓▓ in his Mafter's affections, no
longer thought it incumbent upon him to
obtain for his tricks, the fanction of the
Gentleman's approbation, who fuffered him
ftill to commit, with impunity, every mifchief he fet his heart upon :—But the time
of Pug's difgrace drew nigh ; his fenfes being intoxicated with praifes of his wit and
humour, and the unlimited freedom given
to his wantonnefs, he flew upon his Mafter's fhoulder, and after amufing himfelf,
in jumping with great agility from right to
left, and left to right, he fat fome time confidering what whim he fhould next indulge
himfelf in, and looking on his Mafter with
that contempt which fuch ill-chofen friends
generally feel towards thofe who load them
with obligations they are convinced they
owe more to flattery and their patron's
folly, than to their own intrinfic merit or
his real friendfhip, the fancy took him to
try the extent of his weaknefs, by fnatching
out feveral hairs from his Mafter's whifkers.

Surprife

Surprife, for a moment, kept him filent!
but pain recalling his recollection—anger
and revenge obliterated all rem   nce
of the pleafure Pug had afforded   nd
deprived him of the power of r   g,
that he fhould condemn his own imp   t
indulgence, which was alone in f   ut
giving way to all the impetuofity o   e,
he threw him to the ground, and a   feverely chaftifing him, fpurned him from
him with fury, vehemently forbidding him
ever to prefume to enter into his prefence
more.

M O R A L.

Friendfhip, formed inconfiderately, is a proof
of a weak mind:—Sudden changes, not founded
on fubftantial reafons, mark a levity of difpofition ;—let the great beware !—truth is difficult
for them to find, and the phantoms of affection
and fincerity often attend the coronet. Let the
little alfo reflect, that favorites, who, forget-
ting their dependance, grow fo boldly familiar
as to take improper liberties with their mafters,
may always be fure, fooner or later, of being
driven from their afylum with contempt and
difgrace, fubjected to the fcorn and derifion of
the whole world. ·

VI.

VI, The Lioness and Her Whelp.

As the lives, fortunes, and happiness of Sub-
jects greatly depend upon their Kings, too
much care and attention cannot be em-
ployed in sowing the seeds of virtue and
humanity in their hearts—cultivating in
their minds the love of honor and genero-
sity, and creating in their souls the noble
ambition of distinguishing themselves by
justice and clemency.

FABLE.

A Lioness having, to the great joy of
the forest, presented it with a young
Sovereign, was immediately visited by all
her subjects, who were impatient to shew

their

their loyalty, by an early offer of refpect.
The Mule, ftupidly flow in all his refolves,
and negligent in all his duties, d████d it
till it could no longer be ac███ a
compliment, but rather as a d███le
and inconvenient intrufion, which m████-
terfere with more material engageme█ts.

· Thefe reafons, which were urged to him
as proofs of his being too late, were fo
many incitements to his obftinacy to prefent himfelf before the entrance of the royal cave, with the requeft that he might be
admitted to pay his homage to the young
Prince ; but he was juftly mortified at receiving for anfwer, that he could not be
permitted that honor, as the Lionefs was
engaged in teaching her Son the ufe of his
feet, endeavouring to throw an air of majefty into his gait, and learning him the art
of blending in his deportment, that grace
and dignity fo becoming in a King—fo fafcinating and fo fuccefsful in conciliating the
affections, at the fame time that it never
fails commanding the refpect of his fubjects.

Some days paffed before he made a fecond attempt to fee the Lionefs, when fhe
was again denied to him. On his enqui-
ring what engagements fhe could poffibly
                                    have

have now, a large Dog, who guarded the entrance, replied, fhe was carefully inftruct-ing the Young Prince in the noblenefs of his birth ▓▓▓ fhe at the fame time was re-prefent▓▓ treafon to difgrace, and en-deavouring to roufe his emulation, by re-cording thofe honours which had dignified his line, and to which it is expected his foul will be glorioufly ambitious of adding.

The third time he called, they informed him he had chofen a very improper time, as the Lionefs was employed in that part of her Son's education which was the moft arduous, and of the moft confequence to himfelf and people,—acquainting him how he is to acquire the power of rendering himfelf dreaded by his enemies, and feared, yet loved, by his fubjects;—exerting the utmoft effort of her abilities to engraft in his foul, by precepts and examples, cou-rage without cruelty; humanity without weaknefs; juftice without feverity; and above all, impreffing his mind with a due fenfe of that duty which is impofed upon Princes, of difpenfing rewards and punifh-ments impartially to all.

"Well," faid the Mule, "here is great parade and ceremony indeed in the education

tion of a mere brute! —What a ridiculous af-
fectation of weighty engagements!"—The
Lionefs hearing him grumbling as he was
retiring, faid, loud enough for him to hear,
"that as by great care and attention the
education of young minds, preceptors were
enabled to give ftrength to every natural
virtue, and to root out all the baneful
weeds of vice, too much time could not be
devoted to the arduous tafk of forming the
mind and cultivating the heart of the King
of beafts; but reafons which would be un-
derftood and approved of by others, muft
be perfectly unintelligible to the contemptible faculties of a Mule.

M O R A L.

Thofe, who, being appointed to the facred
truft of fuperintending the education of Princes,
are negligent in ftrictly performing their duty,
fhould be declared enemies to the ftate—to
their king—and to humanity,—and banifhed
fociety, as the underminers of its peace.

VII.

VII. The Ass loaded with FLOWERS, and with DUNG.

Look upon the soft perfume and exquisite beauty of the Rose, as the emblem of Virtue, whose attractions are irresistible; and on the Dung, as that of Vice, hideous, offensive, and disgusting.

FABLE.

A GARDENER, had employed many years in cultivating a garden, and took particular pleasure in rearing all kinds of the most beautiful flowers, and bringing them to the highest perfection. On the day appointed to celebrate the honors of the goddess Flora, when the

young

young men and maidens were obliged to appear in crowns of flowers, and to offer up wreaths and garlands on her altar, he indulged his fancy in forming the choiceft productions of his garden into nofegays, garlands, and various other forms; in which he fucceeded with great tafte and elegance; and putting them in panniers on his Afs, carried them before the temple dedicated to Flora, to expofe them to the village for fale.

¶The Rofes, as he went along, fent forth a perfume fo exquifite, that they acted as a fupernatural attraction, infenfibly drawing after them young and old men and women. The Gardener's fuccefs was beyond his expectations: no fooner were his merchandife feen, but cuftomers prefented themfelves on all fides.

Having difpofed of all his Flowers, and thinking it foolifh to return home empty, he took the opportunity of loading back with Dung; and proceeding on, the Afs was very much furprifed at finding himfelf avoided wherever he paffed, and that thofe who were obliged to travel the fame way, teftified the moft evident marks of difguft and contempt.

At

At a lofs to conjecture the caufe of fo fudden a change, fince the morning, when he was followed by crouds, with every appearance of the moft lively pleafure, he addreffed his mafter, requefting to know the reafon, why, wherever he appeared, the people flew from him with eager hafte, as if meeting him would give them pain : The Gardener foon cleared up the myftery, by informing him, that to the Rofes which he had carried on his back in the morning, that refpect was fhewn, their perfume caufing the delight the whole village teftified on his approach ; but that now, on the contrary, he bore in his panniers a load, the ftench of which rendered him fo very offenfive as to occafion the difgrace and neglect of which he complained.

M O R A L.

Thus a mind, fuffering itfelf to be feduced from the paths of Virtue into thofe of Vice, degrades itfelf into a more infufferable nuifance to the hearts of the good and great, than the Dung can poffibly be to the fenfe of fmelling.

VIII.

VIII. The Eagle and Her Young.

Young Princes who are too self-willed, and too vain to listen to the advice of the wise and experienced, often draw down danger upon their own heads, and destruction on their kingdom.

FABLE.

AN Eagle, mother of two young birds, whom she nursed and fed with great care and tenderness, found herself vehemently importuned by the eldest, to permit him to go in search of prey himself. It was in vain the Eagle represented to him that he was too young; that he had not yet acquired sufficient strength to resist the

attack

tacks, even of the weakeſt of his enemies; and entreated him to reflect, that he could not poſſibly make uſe of his wings, as they were yet ſcarcely fledged.

Deaf to the remonſtances of his Mother, and fluſhed with the ſelf-conceit of youth, he was perſuaded he could, if called upon to exert them, boaſt of courage, ſtrength, and abilities to ſecure him ſucceſs, victory, and fame; and became more earneſt in his requeſt; with which, the old Eagle, finding her arguments unattended to, complied; and, hoping to convince him of the tenderneſs and rationality of her advice, without making him pay too ſeverely for his experience, ſhe took him upon her wings, flying with him, till ſhe came over a meadow, where the herbage was very thick and ſafe; then deſcending within a ſhort diſtance from the ground, ſhe gently launched him into the air, to make his firſt experiment.

His flight was not of long duration; his ſtrength ſoon forſook him—ſoon brought him with violence to the ground; and though not materially hurt, he felt ſufficient pain to make him repent of his raſhneſs, and to promiſe never to make another

ther attempt, till his Mother should pronounce his wings equal to support him: However in a few days after, impatient of controul, and no longer feeling the pain resulting from his first imprudence, he again renewed his importunate request, that his Mother would at least permit him to follow her.

The old Eagle possessing a great deal of wisdom, finding him urge it with all the ardent obstinacy of youth, was apprehensive, that too strict a prohibition would irritate him to rush, with a headlong impetuosity, from his nest, in defiance of her commands; she therefore softened her present refusal, by only postponing a compliance, till her return from seizing some prey, where, from his ignorance of the place, he would rather prevent than facilitate her success; thus soothing him, she obtained from him an assurance that he would not make any effort to go from home during her absence: But she had no sooner taken flight, than a young Vulture, who had overheard the caution, and was bent on mischief, came to him and animated him to take courage, persuaded him he was wise enough to act for himself; and roused his pride by contemptuously ridiculing

culing the abfurd delicacy with which he
was brought up.

Too weak to defpife the irony of an evil
advifer ;—too opiniated to believe his Mother wifer than himfelf, he was ftung to the
quick with an imputation on his ftrength,
and courage, and immediately, forgetful
of his promife to his Mother, quitted his
neft ; but fuffering himfelf to be carried by
the winds, from his ignorance in the art of
guiding and fupporting himfelf by his
wings, he met the fame fate that punifhed
his firft prefumption.

The Eagle hearing his cry, flew to him,
with anxious hafte, and feeing near him,
his imprudent advifer, the Vulture, whom
fhe accufed as the original caufe of the ac-
cident, foon facrificed him to her anger ;
then charging her wings, with her Son
once more, conducted him to his neft, perfectly convinced of his folly ; and an example to his brother, of the painful effects
of imprudence.

M O R A L.

Thofe who difobey the commands of their
parents,—who are obftinately deaf to the dictates of reafon, and fuffer vanity to miflead
them from their duty, will receive the fevereft
of punifhments ; that, which fatal experience
has fuch full power to inflict.

D   IX.

IX. The STORKS and the KITE.

The firſt duty is due to our Parents, even in preference to our Children ; therefore it has pleaſed the Almighty to enforce it, by delivering it as a commandment.

FABLE.

A RICH FARMER, who dealt very large-ly in Cattle, made it a cuſtom to drive his Sheep every night into a Barn, leaving with them the Shepherd, whoſe buſineſs it was to conduct them in the morning to paſture. One day, when this man had ſuſtained a very ſevere wetting from its having rained inceſſantly during the whole
time

time he was attending the Sheep, he found it neceffary, on his return at night, to endeavor to dry his cloathes by making a little fire ; but either unfortunately, or through negligence, the fire communicated itfelf to fome ftraw in a corner of the Barn, and in a few hours confumed it to afhes.

The greateft part of the Sheep luckily efcaped, but fome poor Storks who had built their nefts on the top of the Barn, where they had comfortably and tenderly lodged their aged Father and Mother, as well as their Children, were, by this imprudence of the Shepherd, involved in the greateft diftrefs, and thrown into the moft eminent danger. They found themfelves enveloped in fmoke, which gave them a melancholy prefentiment of the difafter that had happened ; but the Daughter, who was the only one prefent capable of acting, (the Son being abfent) reflecting, with great prefence of mind, that unlefs fhe exerted her fortitude to fubdue her agonifing fears, thofe precious moments would be wafted in vain regrets, that ftill remained to admit hopes of being able to fave, at leaft, fome individual of her beloved family, callied reafon, therefore, to her aid, to ftill the anguifh of her heart,

and following the dictates of virtue,
haftened to take charge of her venerable
Father, determined to filence the yearn-
ings of maternal love, till she had performed her duty to the authors of her being, and placing him on her wings trembl-
ingly bore him to a place of fafety.

Returning, with the eager hopes and
virtuous intent of refcuing her Mother, and
receiving the only confolation the deep
fenfe she had of her misfortune could af-
ford her, (that of being confcious she was
acting right,) she was accofted by a Kite :
who loudly and without referve, addreffed
her, and bluntly reproached her with want
of humanity—of being a difgrace to the
maternal character, and unworthy the
bleffing of poffeffing it ;—feverely condemned her as deftitute of fenfe, as well
as devoid of every amiable fentiment, in
being barbarous enough to facrifice her
Children, and weak enough to refcue, in
preference, two old carcaffes, who could
only be a burthen to themfelves, —a plague
to their friends,—and a nuifance to others ;
and of courfe the fooner they were annihilated the better it would be for all parties.

" I

"I truly love my Children," anfwered the Stork with great philofophy, as fhe haftened her flight, "but I am bound by duty, gratitude, and the decrees of heaven, to give the preference to thofe from whom I derived my exiftence. "The Gods may reward my adherence to their commandment, by bleffing me with more Children; but it is not in Nature to fupply the lofs of a beloved Mother and an eftimable Father. Never,—never fhall any neglect of mine haften that period which I dread,—which will fill me with regret; but which, when it does arrive, from the wife ordination of of Heaven, I fhall fubmit to without repining; and feek confolation in the grief-difpelling reflection; that it was not invited by my want of duty towards them, nor deferved by any fault.

M O R A L.

Indifcretion and negligence, the foibles of youth, is the fource from which many unexpected calamities and misfortunes have fprung.

X. The LION RE-CROWNED.

*A wife Prince ought to be prudent, without
artifice ;—chearful, without degrading
his dignity,—and brave, without cruelty.*

FABLE.

SOME ill-difpofed animals, tired of the
mildnefs, profperity, and peace which
diftinguifhed the reign of a wife old Lion,
whofe juftice and clemency formed a fhield
to guard him from every afperfion, and
from every juft complaint, entered into a
league to depofe him, and knowing that
time, which had ftrengthened his mind
and cultivated to perfect ripenefs every virtue

tue of the heart, had alfo ftamped his fore-head with wrinkles, and enfeebled his limbs with his iron hand, infolently tore the Crown from his venerable brows.

No fooner had they got it into their pof-feffion than their encreafing arrogance made them throw off all kind of refpect to-wards one, whofe great age obliged him to depend upon the allegiance of his fubjects for that duty and obedience, which, when youth ftrung his nerves, and braced his finews to anfwer the dictates of his brave foul, he would have enforced.

The ring-leaders of this rebellion were the Boar, the Fox, and the Monkey. Their treafon, which united them, having fucceeded thus far, felf-intereft began to predominate and to fow the feeds of diffen-fion among them ; each claiming the prize, and appropriating thofe virtues to them-felves, which they thought would beft en-title them to wear it.

The Fox maintained, he was the wifeft, and that for the government of a kingdom great fagacity and prudence were abfolute-ly requifite.

The

The Monkey affirmed, that a Prince fhould be lively, droll, and poffeffed of great humour; therefore he claimed the preference, being abundantly endowed with the power of conciliating, by his entertaining wit, that affection which a King ought to be affured of from his fubjects.

The Boar did not feek to conceal the contempt he felt for the proofs they had both offered as weighty arguments in their favor, fince without ftrength being added to them they would fail of invefting them with that authority without which, it would be impoffible to keep poffeffion of that crown, which weaknefs in their Sovereign, not their bravery, had enabled them to wreft from his head: to which there being a general affent, it was refolved by the affembly to crown the Boar.

The Monkey was appointed to perform that ceremony; but it was found fo ill-fuited, both in fhape and fize, that every endeavour to fix it with fafety, proved vain. "I fee," faid the Fox, "the Gods difapprove of our choice, not doubting but the tyranny of your mind will induce you to facrifice, even the moft faithful of your kingdom, to gratify the cruelty of your nature". They

They then offered the crown to the Fox;
but his head was found much too sharp;
——" And the Gods," answered the Boar,
"expect that kings should act, not with craft,
guile, and cunning; but with justice, honor,
and a generous candour:" "It is the Monkey then who is to govern us," said the af-
sembly at large; but his head was so unstea-
dy, and so capricious in its motions, that
it was so impossible to catch it, even for a
moment, settled enough to try how a crown
would become it; that they all unanimoufly, and with one voice, cried out, "if we
were imprudent enough to elect you King,
the contemptible foolery and ill-timed wag-
gishness of your humor and wit (as you call
it) would not only draw upon you the contempt of the strangers who visited your
court, but expose you to the ridicule of
even your own subjects".

" Therefore," said the wisest, "after this
proof of the folly, as well as criminality of
our conduct, in depriving him of the crown,
to whom the Gods decreed it, we have
no alternative, but, throwing ourselves at
the feet of the Lion,—to acknowledge our
crime,—bewail our imprudence,—and im-
plore his clemency, that he may again re-
store us to his favor;—forget our sincerely-
repented

repented rebellion ; and that He, for whofe head alone the Crown was intended and on whofe facred brows alone it fits with benign majeftic grace, would once more deign to accept it, in confideration of the general welfare and peace of fubjects fo many years muft have endeared to him.

M O R A L.

To acknowledge a Fault as foon as we are convinced it is one, is a generous pride, and reflects an honor that obliterates all remembrances of its ever having been committed ; but a tardy repentance, the effect of difappointed expectations, not of loyal fentiments and a wifh to return to their duty, deferves to be refented with fcorn and punifhed with rigor.

XI.

XI. The WOLF, the ASS, and the LION.

Thofe who are fo devoid of fenfibility and good
temper as to be offended at an error com-
mitted, through an over-anxioufnefs to
pleafe, will undoubtedly prove ungrateful
for the higheft favors, and are defervedly
treated, when perfectly flighted and avoided

F A B L E.

A LION, by nature generous, noble, and
grateful, returning victorious from a
defperate battle, which he had bravely won,
determined to give a grand Feaft to all thofe
who had affifted him in obtaining his con-
queft : Feeling, with that liberality attached
to

to real bravery, that he fhould lofe half the delight of even boafting the glorious title of conqueror, if thofe who had fhared the dangers of acquiring his laurel-crown did not alfo fhare the horror and the booty which attended it; he invited them all to meet in a large meadow; where he provided food of all kinds to fuit the different palates of his vifitors, anxious that nothing fhould be wanting to make it, indifcriminately, agreeable to all parties.

Before the repaft took place he condefcended to return them thanks for their fervices,—praifed the zeal they had fhewn by the animated fupport they had afforded him in the dangers he had encountered,—and defired, as a proof how fenfible he was of their fidelity, that they would partake of the entertainment he had prepared for them.

Happy in their Prince's favor and flattered by his gracious praifes, all, in great fpirits, immediately accepted his invitation, except the Afs and the Wolf; who never ceafed grumbling, that the Lion fhould have been fo particularly inattentive to them as not to provide thiftles for the one, and carrion for the other, unlefs he had intended to take this opportunity of publicly affronting them.

The

The Lion, who was fenfible that (tho' he omitted thiftles and carrion,) there were at the feaft many other things on which they could very delicioufly regale themfelves, & looking upon their complaints as the effect of a difcontented, ungrateful, and unfatisfied difpofition, efteemed them both beneath his anger or his notice ; and, without paying the leaft regard to their murmurs, gave himfelf up to the gratification of remarking the pleafure and content, with which the others partook of his munificence.

The Monkey relifhed the nuts,—the Dog with great glee, feized upon fome meat,—the Bull enjoyed the hay,—the Horfe feafted plentifully upon corn,—and the Elephant was perfectly fatisfied with bread. Thus all returned home cheerful, happy, and grateful for the pleafure the Lion had condefcended to give them.

M O R A L.

The vicious avoid the fociety of the amiable ; and the amiable are incapable of taking pleafure in an intercourfe with the depraved in Morals.

XII.

XII. The ORANGE, and other TREES.

Thofe who are elevated to rank, fortune, and power, fhould be diftinguifhed for the virtue and purity of their lives, and their cha-racters dignified by acts of liberality to-wards others whofe fituation calls for the exertion of the foftening hand of humanity to relieve (perhaps undeferved) calamities. If fuch be the conduct of a man in private life, we may depend upon his fupporting a public one with juftice, honor, and mild-nefs.

FABLE.

THE Trees having frequently remark-ed, that Birds acknowledged the Eagle

as

as their king, and that the Lion was no lefs
refpected as ' a fovereign by every other
beaft came to a refolution of raifing to that
dignity, one among themfelves, to whom all
the other Trees fhould pay homage, and in
whom fhould be vefted full power to exercife every royal prerogative.

A meeting, therefore, was appointed to
receive the different candidates ; to hear
their different pretenfions, and to decide
the important queftion of "who is moft
worthy ?"

Claimants, as may be fuppofed, flocked
from all quarters ; fome led by ambition,
others by pride; but thofe introduced by
folly and felf-love, were innumerable:
Thefe various conductors did not fail to
flatter them on their way, with the infin-
cerity of fycophants, that they had every
juft title to the envied rank they afpired to:
But, when arrived at the meeting they
began to exhibit their pretenfions to virtues which none but themfelves ever allowed them ; and to boaft of abilities, of which
(themfelves excepted) all were ignorant ;
a general murmur of difapprobation mark-
ed the prudence of retiring from an
affembly, which by a longer ftay therein,
they

they might irritate to a more infulting rc-
jettion.

Every infignificant candidate, by this
means, being difcarded, there was full lei-
fure to enquire into the merits of five or fix;
whofe claims appearing to be fanftioned by
reafon, gave them a right to a generous in-
veftigation, an impartial attention, and a
ftrong exertion of all the powers of a juft
difcrimination.

The Oak ftood foremoft, recommending
itfelf to the dignity, by the wifdom and experience, it cannot fail of acquiring, and
improving, in a life of incredible length ;
—by the protettion it was capable of affording under its fpacious branches, which was
almoft as boundlefs as the fuccour it's rich
Acorns enabled him to beftow, and to which
men of the higheft rank and moft diftinguifhed charafters had been indebted for the
prefervation of their lives ; and that, however vain and affuming the boaft might appear, he was too nobly ambitious of being
thought worthy of the crown, to omit adding, that he had had the honorable title confered on him, of being the bulwark of king-
doms :—the juft right he had to that dif-
ftinftion, he fubmitted to the candour of
the committee.

Sc.

So much reafon, majefty, and truth, appeared in this fpeech, that it was received with unanimous applaufe; but was filenced by an addrefs from the Laurel, who beg'd them to take into confideration the great favor in which he was held by the Gods who had thought him worthy of having beftowed on him the wonderful and unparalleled virtue of withftanding the dreadful effects of thunder and lightening, and guarding, from its deftructive power, the terrified and unprotected traveller.

" To my rank no objection can be made," faid he, " fince I have, for ages, been e-fteemed the emblem of eternal fame to the glorious deeds of heroes;—of the eternal admiration due to great and fublime abilities;—and have had the honor of encircling the brows of the moft diftinguifhed of the Roman Emperors, who would have thought the celebration of their triumphs (on their returning victorious) as wanting half its dignity—half its brilliancy, had not a crown formed of my leaves, on their entering the capitol, adorned their heads.

Various fentiments were created by this addrefs of the Laurel; but the generality, though they refpected the gift confered on him by the Gods, thought him too vain of the diftinction paid him by men who had loaded him with honors, more from caprice, than any fuperior merit he poffeffed over other Evergreens.

The Pomegranate was the next who offered; depending that two reafons, he fhould propofe, would fpeak very forcibly in his favor, he began his argument with confidence: The one was, that the regularity with which his feed was arranged, was a fign of the union he fhould be able to preferve among his fubjects, which muft ever be deemed one of the ftrongeft duties of a King; the other was, that the crown which nature had beftowed upon him, evidently fhewed fhe had not only thought him deferving of a kingdom, but had defigned that he fhould one day hold the reins of government.

His firft argument was admitted, but his fecond being founded on the fhallow bafis of perfonal advantages, the affembly waited in filence for the Olive to urge his fuit; which he fupported by the ftrong recommendation of being the fymbol of peace, and the favorite of the goddefs Minerva, to whom he was confecrated.

But

But the Vine, above all, loudly maintained; that man owed to him the prolongation of a life which, at the moſt advanced age, they were weak enough to reſign with regret; and to preſerve which, for one hour, they would reſign all the luxuries the boaſted virtues of his competitors could beſtow.

The Olive did not want for amiable qualities, therefore had made himſelf ſome intereſt in the minds of his judges; but he was ſo devoid of thoſe ſtriking ones which ſhould mark the character of Princes, that he was paſſed by with regret. The Vine was, with all his brilliant qualities and virtues, rejected; as being the cauſe of more ruin and deſtruction than he was capable of good.

They therefore began to find themſelves extremely puzzled, on whom they ſhould fix to fill the elevated rank they were aſſembled to confer; when all eyes were ſuddenly attracted to the Orange, who waited in modeſt ſilence to hear the deciſion of the judges:—unaſſuming, he neither ſought for rank or power, and ſeemed inſenſible to the innumerable virtues—the many intrinſic merits and advantages which appeared to others ſo conſpicuouſly deſigned to add grace to the Crown, rather than to receive dignity from it.

E2.   Surpriſed

Surprifed they fhould have hefitated fo long!—His very rivals turned advocates for him, fenfible of thofe well-grounded reafons which could not fail to influence all minds in chufing him as their Sovereign; and though he declined making any pretenfions to the empire, the affembly unanimoufly elected him their King; warmly fetting forth the juftice of his claims, which muft be indifputable, as they were founded on the perpetual verdure of his leaves, a fign that his mind when arrived at maturity, would ftill retain all the vigour of youth,—that the incomparable perfume of his flowers was an emblem of the fweets or comforts, which arife from a virtuous life, both to ourfelves and others,— and above all, that his fruits, fit to gather at all feafons, proved that boundlefs and unalterable liberality, which fhould mark the character of every monarch, amiably defirous of being efteemed the father of his people.

M O R A L.

Thofe who rule fhould make it the principal ftudy of their hearts, and bufinefs of their lives, to gain the affection, efteem, and admiration of their fubjects; drawing them by thofe endearing ties to feel duty light, and obedience pleafing.

XIII.

XIII.   The ERMINE and the PRINCE.

We are frequently indebted to the liberality of
strangers for acts of kindness and genero-
sity, which the insensibility or avarice of
those, from whom we had a right to expect
them, have denied us.

FABLE.

AN ERMINE, finding that being the
youngest of a large family deprived
him of all distinction, and that his elder
brothers engrossed all that attention and respect which was equally due to his birth, entreated his mother to permit him to travel.
Her penetration soon discovered the reason,
and though she was by no means devoid of

       sensibility

fenfibility or affection towards him; yet the difguft he had taken againft his country proceeding from juft provocation, fhe did not attempt to diffuade him from a refolution her. prudence fuggefted was likely to contribute both to his happinefs and eftablifhment. She therefore, not only gave her free confent, but expreffed her approbation, and promoted the execution of his plan, by informing him, that a relation of his had lately left his friends from the fame motive, and with the fame fanguine hopes, which had been fortunately realifed. Notwithftanding this feparation was by mutual confent, many tears teftified the regret they felt at its being neceffary.

The Ermine purfued his journey all through Flanders, but finding nothing but neglect and indifference, he proceeded as far as France ; then did he experience a reverfe of fortune indeed ! To that philanthropy, the french are famed for fhewing towards ftrangers, was added the higheft admiration wherever he appeared : Charmed with the enchanting beauty of his fkin they could not refrain from touching it, or keep their eyes from the brilliant whitenefs fo peculiar to that animal, and which was fo furprifing, as left them at a lofs which to admire moft, its exquifite colour, or its delightful texture.

Being

Being arrived at Paris, the parifian fame foon founded the praifes of the Ermine in the ears of the monarch himfelf, who immediately ordered him to appear before his throne. It was then he became fenfible, that he might fafely indulge every ambitious hope,—it was then he found his former moft fanguine expectations fall very far fhort of the honors and happinefs that awaited him;—flattered, careffed, and refpected,—encreafing in favor every day, his heart overflowed with joy, and in extacy, he exclaimed, "thrice happy departure from my native land!—Oh! bleffed be the hour in which I thought of quitting an ungrateful country, to meet with fuch unbounded friendfhip, from the greateft and moft deferving of princes,—to meet with diftinctions and favors which more than compenfate,—which greatly overpay me for all the contempt I experienced in my own nation."

M O R A L.

A Mother fhould exert her fortitude to fubdue every felfifh tendernefs which interferes with the welfare of her children.—France is worthy of imitation in ever having diftinguifhed itfelf above other nations, by generoufly offering her arms as a refuge and an afylum to diftreffed merit, or to unfortunate princes.

XIV. A NOBLEMAN and his HOUND.

A good reputation,—a noble character, may defy the scythe of time, or the shafts of adversity : for the truly amiable, will ever pay the highest respect to virtue, under whatever form she may think proper to present herself.

FABLE.

A NOBLEMAN passing near a dunghill, as he was going to the chace, perceived an old Hound lying upon it, but so thin, and in so dreadful a condition from the bad treatment she had for some time

met

met with, that it was impoſſible for him to
recollect her: ſtruck with compaſſion at
the ſight of her emaciated form, which ſtill
retained traces of her former beauty, he
remained ſome time regarding her with an
eye of pity, which the poor brute perceiving, wagged her tail in gratitude for his
humane attention, and raiſing her head as
if deſirous of ſaying ſomething intereſting,
ſhewed a countenance in which was painted the moſt earneſt entreaties for protection,—the moſt evident proofs of deſerving
it,—and the ſtrongeſt marks of that un-
merited wretchedneſs, which claims aſſiſt-
ance from every feeling heart.

Still encouraged by the countenance of
the young Lord, ſhe exerted her little re-
maining ſtrength, and dragged in agony,
her wounded body to the feet of the Nobleman, who in admiration of the fortitude
which had enabled her, notwithſtanding
her debilitated ſtate, to leave her dunghill, received her with the moſt heart-re-
viving careſſes, which gave the poor animal reſolution to addreſs him in the following words,

"I perceive, my Lord, that the filth
with which I am covered—the poverty

to which I am reduced—and the broken thigh, under which misfortune I endure tortures, and which forever deprives me of the power of fhewing you that zeal I have hitherto evinced in your fervice, form, altogether, a difguife which robs me of that place in your memory I was formerly fo happy in poffeffing, under the name of *Fair Maid*, whofe reputation in the chace was unrivalled,—in whofe glory you took the greateft pride, and whofe fame was thought worthy of interefting the royal ear".

" It was I, (forgive the vanity of this re-trofpeétion) who feized that wonderful Stag that had fo often been unfuccefsfully hunt-ed in the foreft of *Compeigne;* but what I more particularly pride myfelf upon,—what even at this time, when I am fuffering the moft acute pain—my fpirits depreffed with the fevereft calamities—and my body weakened by poverty, has power to af-fwage my diftrefs, and make me forget I am no longer young or happy, is, that on that day !—that glorious day ! I was accompanied by forty dogs who owed to me their exiftence—whom I could own without a blufh, and whofe fame prevent-ed mine from fading, even in age",—

If

" If your highnefs has any doubts of the
truth of my affertions, I will take the liberty of refering you to your Gallery, in
which you will, by the colour of my fkin,
and its marks, (all that remain of my former qualities) find me at the head of my
children, leading them to the chace and to
the victory, I have already defcribed, and
on that proof I reft my hopes of receiving
comfort and affiftance".

Her ftrength failed her, and in filence
fhe waited the fuccefs of an application on
which her life depended. The Nobleman,
who was paffionately fond of the chace, and
of courfe attached to his dogs and horfes,
immediately recollected the circumftances
fhe had been recounting, which recalled
to his mind the figure of this faithful, worthy old fervant, and created in him the
tendereft pity,—revived all the affection
he had once felt for his favorite, and made
him look back with regret on that inattention, on his part, which had reduced the
poor creature to fo abject, fo miferable a
ftate : Renewing, therefore, the kindeft
and moft confoling careffes, he delivered
her to his vallet, with orders to 'take the
tendereft care of her,—to wafh her with
warm water,—have a proper perfon to
cure

cure her leg, and to bring her every day
to his table, to receive her meat from her
Lord's hands ; and, that he might be convinced, by conftantly feeing her, that fhe
had that attention paid her, which he was
determined fhe fhould enjoy for the remain-
nder of her life.

As they were carrying her home, another old dog who had been a witnefs of the
gracious reception which had been given
her, and the kindneffes which were the re-
fult of her petition, thought he would not
lofe fo fair an opportunity of being equally
fortunate ; he therefore, in an abrupt addrefs, put in his claim for equal confideration, endeavoring to fupport his pretenfions, by boafting of his long fervices,—
his poverty, and his age : but thefe pretenfions not being fupported by truth, and
the Nobleman knowing his fervices had
been few,—his abilities below mediocrity,
and that his poverty proceeded more from
idlenefs, which made him fly his kennel,
than from the feeblenefs of age, mounted
his horfe and followed the chace.

M O R A L.

It is a duty (which every heart, poffeffed of
fenfibility, muft fulfil with pleafure) to fup-
                                            port

port thofe in age, who have devoted their
youth to your fervice : The dependent fituation of the perfons who have been faithfully attached to your intereft, does not excufe you
from a gratitude which fhould be teftified on
every opportunity of fmoothing the down-hill
of their lives, and promoting (what muft be
ftill more dear to them) the happinefs of thofe
whom they may chance to leave unprotected
and unconfoled ; but by the hope that a parent's merit may give them a claim on your
generofity.

XV.

XV. The LION, the SHEEP, and the WOLF,

*Thofe only deferve power, who generoufly
exert it in defending the helplefs.*

FABLE.

A LION returning from battle, by a private path, that he might convey the rich booty he had gained with more fafety, difcovered at fome diftance, a fheep flying with all the fpeed that her ftrength (being breathlefs with fright) would permit. Sufpecting fhe was endeavouring to efcape fome dreaded enemy, the Lion thought to give her courage by calling to her, and
offering

offering his protection; but the Sheep terrified beyond the power of difcrimination,
and too fenfible of her weaknefs to hope
for any fafety but in flight, redoubled, without daring to look behind, the fpeed of
her trembling fteps, which gave the Lion
reafon to think that the Wolf could not be
far behind.

He foon found himfelf right in his con-
jectures, by perceiving through the trees,
that cruel beaft, to all appearance, in eager purfuit on the fame tract his poor innocent prey had traced ; and feeling the
noble impulfe of counteracting the Wolf's
inhuman intentions, he made a fhort cut
to ftop him in his career, addreffing him
coldly with the queftion, what caufe could
poffibly require his travelling fo faft, and
with fo much impatience ?——" Hunger",
anfwered the Wolf, "which has obliged
me to leave my cave to go in queft of
wherewithal to fatisfy it".

" If that be your only bufinefs", replied the Lion, " do not be at the trouble
or fatigue of continuing your uncertain
purfuit, but partake with me of a rich
booty which will fufficiently gratify your
palate, and filence the cravings of your
ftomach".

The

The Wolf, who would much rather have followed the delicious prey he had in view, was at a lofs how to excufe himfelf from accepting the Lion's invitation; but after a fhort hefitation he perceived it was impoffible to refufe it, without difcovering his cruel intentions; which were become ftill more cruel, as neceffity could no longer be admitted as a plea, after the generous offer that had been made him; he, therefore, partly through policy, and partly through fear, confented with a grace (he thought unfufpected) to follow the Lion, who proceeded with all that chearfulnefs which the confcioufnefs of having done a good action, never fails to infpire.

Being arrived at his den, he placed every thing that the greateft glutton could require, before the Wolf, who inwardly grumbled at every mouthful, fancying what he poffeffed far inferior to the prey he had been obliged to forego; becaufe in the fheep he would not only have fatiated his hunger, but have given the higheft enjoyment to the barbarous delight his mind took in cruelty: while the Lion, on the contrary, felt inexpreffible pleafure, in having, by his addrefs, given the Sheep time to efcape, and by his generofity, fucceeded in appeafing the fury of the Wolf.

MORAL

M O R A L.

Many Misfortunes may be prevented by a
well-timed exertion of liberality and courage.

F   XVI.

XVI. The Peacock and Ibis.

How many there are, who from poſſeſſing an engaging perſon, inſinuating manner, and a lively turn for converſation, make ſo deep an impreſſion on you at firſt ſight, as to create a deſire of improving the acquaintance into a friendſhip ; but who, on a more ſcrutiniſing enquiry, prove themſelves either mere ſuperficial characters, or elſe unworthy of eſteem, from their vices, and dangerous from that art which enabled them to impoſe themſelves upon your credulity as being no leſs amiable, than agreeable.

FABLE.

A Peacock, being ambitious of gaining as general a reputation for pru-

dence

dence in the choice of a friend, as he already poffeffed for unrivaled beauty, determined to travel in fearch of fuch a one, as fhould reflect honor upon his underftanding, and from whom he might, at the fame time derive a conftant fource of pleafure. His exterior charms had the power of attracting even the notice of the Eagle, who offered to enter into a ftrict amity with him ; but he thought it was afpiring too high to become the companion of his mafter, well knowing, that no friendfhip can be of long duration where there is a great inequality in rank.

The Goldfinch and the Nightingale pleafed him well enough; the one on account of its fweet note, and the other for its beautiful plumage ; but he felt that he fhould be afhamed of being feen in their company, from the infignificance of their figure. The Parrot was too great a tatler :—The Oftrich was as ftupid in mind as he was heavy in body :—The Hawk was too cruel, and the Vulture equally as unamiable.

As he was begining to think of returning, (for he had already reached as far as *Egypt*, he perceived on the borders of the

Nile, a large Bird, fomewhat refembling, in fhape, the Stork, but poffeffing all its merits, without its defects. Its plumage was a beautiful fhining black; its beak long and hooked, and, as well as his legs, of a fine red ;—it was called an Ibis, and added to the above advantages, "his maje- ftic mein and air, attracted the notice of the Peacock, who immediately advanced towards him with the moft friendly over- tures of acquaintance with him.

The Ibis was ftruck with the richnefs and beauty of the Peacock's tail, which drew from him, as much, or indeed, more refpect, than he would have paid, even to the Eagle himfelf. For two hours they en- joyed the greateft fatisfaction imaginable in each others fociety, and each congratu- lated himfelf in a meeting which promifed to be productive of fo much ferene happi- nefs to both parties.

The Peacock began to think himfelf overpaid for the trouble of fo long a jour- ney, and there was every appearance of the ftricteft and moft unalterable friendfhip taking place, when the Ibis plunging his long neck into the Nile, and drawing it back full of water, conveyed it through his

bill

bill, in a dirty manner, into his body.
The Peacock was aftonifhed and difgufted;
all his favourable opinion of him vanifhed,
and unable to reftrain his indignation, he
burft out into the fevereft reproaches ;—
" thou filthy beaft !—How have I difgrac-
ed myfelf by converfing with thee !—Piti-
ful, bafe, unworthy wretch !—artful vil-
lain ! who can affume the outward appearance of honor, dignity, and worth; and
whofe interior is the feat of obfcenity,
meannefs, and vice !"

And immediately taking wing, he was
retiring, when his flight was arrefted by the
voice of the Ibis, who thus broke his con-
temptuous filence—" Thus am I punifhed
for fuffering myfelf to be attracted by your
gaudy plumage, without confidering how
much I degraded myfelf by even thinking
of forming a friendfhip with one who is but
the offspring of pride and folly.—What are
your boafts, vain bird? but that you
are painted and trifling as the Butterfly—
and your beauty fhort-lived as the Rofe?—
And will you dare to vie with me, who
am of fuch effential fervice to my country,
as to have had divine honors paid me?—
To convince you of the weaknefs of taking difguft (which ignorance is apt to do)

at

at what it is beyond your comprehenfion to account for,—know, that in the circum-ftance you took offence at, I merely fol-lowed the inftinct nature has endowed me with, and from. which I find relief againft every complaint my fpecies is fubject to : and what ftill adds to my fame and fuperi-ority, over fuch an infignificant bird as you, is, that the fame circumftance was the means of teaching that noble creature man a new method of rendering medicine of fervice to his fellow-creatures.

"What have you done, either for the fer-vice of your own kind, or for the nobleft work of God ?——What are your virtues ? —Retire in fhame at your prefumption, and with regret that you have loft a friend, who would have confered an honor on you, it is not in your power to beftow ".—— The Peacock once more took wing with a drooping creft.

M O R A L.

It is wifdom to fly from folly ;—it is virtue to fhun the vicious : but unlefs you are indul-gent to foibles, feek not a friend, for you are not yourfelf without faults,—perfection is in-compatible with our nature.

XVII

XVII. The DUEL between the RAT and the FROG.

There are very few provocations which can justify the having recourse to a revenge that endangers the life of a fellow-creature; and we have a right to believe that person possessed of a heart filled with envy, malice, cruelty, and every vice baneful to society, who, for every trifling offence, flies to his sword for redress.

FABLE.

AN Elephant and a Rhinoceros, after having had very frequent and very violent quarrels, met in a large meadow,
F4   when

when the latter found himſelf very much
puzzled how to invent ſome charge againſt
the Elephant, which, bearing the colour
of reaſon, might in ſome meaſure juſtify
his having been the aggreſſor in all their diſ-
putes; and endeavoring to make the loud-
neſs of his reproaches ſtand in lieu of the
juſtice of them, he began in a hoſtile manner, to enumerate the faults which he
thought would vindicate the reſentment he
had ſhewn towards the Elephant.

" You have been diſcovered", continued
the Rhinoceros, "attempting, againſt in-
ſtinct,—againſt nature, to infringe on the
peculiar prerogative of man, by practiſing
with a ſword to obtain an undue advantage
over your adverſaries. You are alſo accuſ-
ed of conſulting the heavens, and ſtudying
the ſtars, to learn whether you will ever be
able to ſucceed in your rebellious deſigns
of uſurping the throne; for which purpoſe
alſo, you have been caught tracing on ｜the
ſand, characters which are ſuſpected of being cabaliſtical, and of black intent".

" If", anſwered the Elephant, " I am
able to wield the ſword, I deſerve praiſe
for my addreſs, in acquiring an art that
may render me as ſerviceable to the ſtate,

as

as in your hands it would be detrimental, suppofing your courage and fkill equal to the badnefs of your heart : Neither am I deferving of cenfure for raifing my eyes to heaven, fince inftinct prompts all who pof- fefs grateful hearts, to offer up daily thankf- givings, for the benefits they have receiv- ed, and I feel a particular impulfe of gra- titude for the rich qualities with which all my race are endowed ; and my writing on the fand, is an evident proof, that my mind is not as dull, as the heavinefs of my bo- dy would fuggeft, fince I am able to exe- cute the moft wonderful of all inventions : But I have not entered into this juftificati- on for the fake of avoiding a battle, from which I by no means wifh or intend to fhrink".

Upon which he raifed his probofcis, as a fignal, to begin the fight, which was an- fwered by the other prefenting his horn, when they were prevented from begining the attack, by the extraordinary fight of a duel between a Rat and a Frog. They had, each of them, armed themfelves with a fharp pointed bulrufh, and were reared on their hinder legs ; in this attitude they were feeking revenge with all the fury of which they were capable.

"Let

" Let us hear the fubjeét of this quarrel"
faid the Rhinoceros, (who had not much
inclination for fighting, and therefore had
no objeétion to poftponing it a little) to
which the Elephant confenting, their curi-
ofity was foon gratified to their own fhame.

" I maintain", cried the Rat, " that a
moufe-coloured grey is the moft beautiful".
—" And I", faid the other, " will not fuffer the green of the Frog to yield in beauty
to the dirty grey of the Rat"; whereupon
they renewed their blows with redoubled
fury:—But the Elephant had heard enough
to cover him with confufion; and turning
towards his antagonift, he thus addreffed
him with concern.

" How much reafon have we to blufh
with fhame, at having condefcended to
meet for the purpofe of gratifying our animofity, and deciding our quarrel in the
fame manner, that thefe wretched infeéts—
thefe abortive produétions of nature, fettle
their contemptible differences; who think
to fcreen their own infignificance, by
imitating the actions of the moft noble
beafts. We will return, and look on this
tranfaétion, as a burlefque, our folly has
deferved".

" In

" In truth", faid the Rhinoceros, "we cannot, after what we have witneffed, fight with honor; therefore I will retire with you, as a friend, for never fhall it be faid we ended our quarrels after the manner of fuch defpicable animals, as Rats and Frogs".

M O R A L.

It is time that men of honor and rank fhould wipe off that ftain from the fword, with which every lacquey and hair-dreffer has of late dared to pollute it. Let the great employ it in the fervice of their country; not difgracing it by drawing it in the caufe of drunken quarrels, or tavern broils. Let them not, for one hafty word, facrifice their own happinefs, and perhaps involve a whole family in ruin, by taking away the life of their only protector and friend, while they deprive the world of an ufeful member of fociety.

XVIII

XVIII.   The Fig and the Olive.

We cannot think it extraordinary, that men
should feel antipathy towards each other,
when we have so many instances, not only
of the inveteracy of beasts to some of their
species, but of trees; who often feel the most
irreconcilable hatred against their neigh-
bour, that it is possible even for the noble
creature man to be sensible of.

FABLE.

A Circumstance, proving the above
assertion, occured, which gave occasion to the Pomegranate to exert that milk
of human kindnefs, for which it is formed,

and

and which agreeing with its exterior qualities, has given it the title of the emblem of
peace and concord.

With an amiable zeal, he attempted to
footh the anger and remove the difguft,
which fubfifted between two near neighbours, the Olive and the Fig : In vain he
exerted every effort of his eloquence to induce them, as fate had deftined them to
live fo near each other, to bury in oblivion
their animofity, and to eftablifh a friendly
intercourfe with each other, which fhould
be a mutual pleafure, and a mutual comfort.

Finding their hearts fhut againft that argument, he affailed their pride and emulation, by bringing numberlefs examples of
other trees living near each other in the
greateft harmony, and exchanging, as opportunity offered, reciprocal acts of kindnefs; which not being able to follow, muft
fubject them to the fevereft cenfure and the
moft public difapprobation. But the Pomegranate found their minds as deaf to the
dictates of reafon, as their hearts were infenfible to the inftigations of friendfhip.

Various were the methods which the
                                    Pomegranate

Pomegranate (never indolent where there is a profpect of doing good) effayed to bring about a reconciliation, but obftinacy baffled all his good intents, and deprived his eloquence of the power it deferved to poffefs. Still too anxious in doing good, to be eafily difcouraged, after having tried every other means, he had recourfe to fevere reproaches, which he addreffed to the Fig, declaring him the aggreffor, in having taken an unjuft, and malicious antipathy towards the Olive, whofe peaceable difpofition was well known, and would of courfe throw the cenfure on him alone.

The Fig, offended at having all the imutation of litigioufnefs thrown upon him, immediately entered upon his juftification, by reprefenting the hatred between their families, which had fubfifted fo long, as to become hereditary, and that it was incompatible with their natures, ever to be upon friendly terms.

" But", continued the Fig, " without entering into a difcuffion of circumftances, which are hid from your view, I will only beg you to judge, by exterior marks, of the contraft which diftinguifhes my character from his, and places a bar of enmity
between

between us and concord : My leaves are large and fcolloped; thofe of the Olive are fhort, and in one piece :—Mine are enamelled with a beautiful green; his are of a dead whitifh green :—My fruit is large and noble; his are pitifully fmall. The colour of the one is a faint refemblance of green ; the other, approaches nearer to purple : —Figs are fweet, and of a grateful flavor ; the Olive is four, and bitter : In fhort the roots, rind, and trunk, differ fo much, that the only good office you can poffibly do us, is to remove us from each other, which can alone prevent quarrels; for though even at a diftance, we can never be friends, we fhall, at leaft, ceafe to be enemies".

M O R A L.

It is vain to attempt reconciling two perfons, whofe difference of fentiment, difpofition, and rank, make it abfolutely impoffible for them to admit the fame pleas, or underftand the fame reafons. The wifh of promoting concord, is natural to the amiable ; but fuccefs, as in the above cafe, is fo doubtful, that the moft prudent method is, when they appear inveterate, to remove them from each other : that near neighbourhood may not tempt them to dangerous acts of revenge, which abfence might both prevent, and mitigate.

XIX

XIX. The EAGLE's NEST.

*Every thing belonging to princes, should be
superb, magnificent, and noble, to engage
reverence from their own subjects,—to im-
press strangers with respect, and enemies
with awe;—and to encourage the greatest
political ornaments of a kingdom; the arts
and sciences.*

FABLE.

THE EAGLE, being soon expected to
lay her eggs, was visited by a number
of birds, who, with just respect. represented to her Majesty, that the Nest she had
chosen was not suitable to her high rank,
and

and that many of the birds afforded themfelves Nefts much fuperior in every refpect;
fome of them lodging themfelves in the
moft magnificent palaces, frequently chufing the chamber, or fome other of the
rooms belonging to the greateft princes;
therefore they befeeched her Majefty to
confider that however amiable moderation
was in a private character, it bore a different
title in fo elevated a ftation, and would
draw upon her the imputation of wanting
that greatnefs which fhould not only
accompany all the actions of Princes, but
fhine through every thing that belonged to
them.

The Eagle gracioufly thanked them for
their advice, which fhe condefcended to
receive as a mark of their loyal affection,
but anfwered, that fhe fhould not change
the place, where fhe had been accuftomed
to lay her eggs, which was either in the
hollow of a large tree, or on the point of
fome high rock; a choice which prudence
had fuggefted, as much for the prefervation
of her young, as the good government of
her people, over whom fhe had an unbounded view from her prefent fituation,
the advantages of which they muft be too
fenfible of to perfift in wifhing her to
G   change

change it ; but if their generofity, loyalty, and affection, prompted them to exert their abilities in rendering it more magnificently fuitable to the diftinguifhed rank of queen of the birds, fhe fhould feel happy in find ing herfelf fo dear to her fubjects ; and grateful for that proof of their zeal and fidelity.

The fwallow and king's-fifher, with great joy and chearfulnefs, received, as a flattering teftimony of favour, this gracious acceptance of their fervices, and began the foundation, in which they followed that plan, which nature, through their inftinct, had taught them, as moft proper for their peculiar kind, building with a firmnefs and ftrength, capable of refifting rain, wind, and ftorms. The Goldfinch, no lefs delighted than the former, with the permiffion, brought, as an offering, his gaudy plumes of red and yellow to embellifh the outfide. The Peacock with princely liberality, laid at her feet his brilliant and beautiful feathers. The Pidgeon's varigated ones were alfo accepted, The Parroquette prefented his lively green ones. The Cock fupplied her with white. The Hern with black, and the Lark with the fofteft cotton, to contribute to the warmth and comfort of the young Eagles.

MORAL

M O R A L.

A prince's firſt ſtudy ſhould be to deſerve,
and thus ſhould ſubjeĉts aĉt and feel ; and, by
a mutual interchange of ſervices and gratitude,
reſtore again, the golden agè.

G2   XX.

XX. The Two Colts.

The vanity of youth, which leads them to set
too high a value upon themselves, often
draws them into difficulties and quarrels
with those, who, equally impetuous, think
it neceſſary to punish boaſtings, which by
appearing to place themselves in an infe-
rior light, rouse their pride and indig-
nation.

FABLE.

TWO young Colts, of very promiſing
expectations, had been placed in
the ſame field, and conſtantly grazed
together in great friendſhip and harmony;
one day after having regaled themſelves
moſt

moft plentifully, one of them was heard to addrefs his companion in the following words: "I cannot imagine what can be the caufe of it, but fince I have feafted upon this herbage I feel myfelf poffeffed of fo much courage, ftrength, and intrepidity, that if you could boaft as much bravery, I believe we fhould, together, be equal to a contest with a powerful army."

The other, who was of a vigorous animated fpirit, replied, that if he were inclined to try their ftrength at any exercife, he would foon convince him what he was capable of; and fmiling, he gave him a blow on the head with his tail, which the firft returned with a quicknefs bordering on impatience. The other, who fought to amufe himfelf, and to enjoy a little mirth, continued fkilfully ftriking him with his long tail, when one of the hairs getting loofe ftuck in the eye of the former, and turned their play into a quarrel; and whether it were from the pain of his eye, or that he was tired of a play in which he had not the fuperiority is not known; but turning his back, he began, in fury, a ferious conteft, lafhing his heels at him with fuch violence and paffion as foon made the other find it neceffary to defend himfelf;

and

and he turning about likewife, they gave
themfelves up to all the rage of offended
pride, envy, and revenge; nor did they
ceafe fighting till he who had began the
quarrel, was difabled from continuing it,
by a dangerous wound in the fhoulder.
Thus ended their friendfhip, and the offen-
der was punifhed by his mafter's configning
him to the dogs, he being no longer fit for
fervice, or worthy the care and attention
to which his high blood, and promifing
qualities would have entitled him.

M O R A L.

What a reflection it is upon the heart and
underftanding of a perfon to fuffer a trifle to
part him from a friend.—But it fo often hap-
pens, that even young people have, very early
in life, an opportunity of feeing from example,
how neceffary it is to correct thofe acids in the
temper, which act like fecret enemies to their
peace, and to be as much upon their guard
againft them, as againft paffion, which makes
a bold and open attack.

XXI

XXI.   The OLD GENTLEMAN, and his TREES.

The praise, which you bestow on a worthy man, strengthens his affection and friend-ship, without encreasing his vanity ; and it is a tribute due to those who have proved themselves zealous in your service.

FABLE.

AN OLD GENTLEMAN, who had dedi-cated the prime of his life to the ser-vice of his prince, and who had diftinguifh-ed himfelf both as a foldier, and as a ftatef-man, finding his mind become unequal to the weight of the one, and his body too enervated to fupport the fatigue of the other, refigned all his employments, and entirely dropping a public chara&er, re-tired into the country with an uncorrupted heart, and as great a fhare of philanthropy as if he had never quitted it.

In the cultivation of his eftates, and in his beautiful gardens he found a guard a-gainft that languor, which generally attends fuch fudden tranfitions ; making them as much an employment, as an amufement, he foon found, that every fhrub and every flower, acquired an interefting claim upon him, and, naturally grateful, he felt him-felf obliged to his trees for the fruit they had fupplied him with.

Walking with fome friends round his gardens, he could not help exprefling to them, the pleafure and peace he enjoyed in a country life, and pointing out to them the variety of beauties which fucceed each other, as a conftant fource of amufement and an inexhauftible fubje& for refle&ion : —"Do you not", faid he, "admire this beautiful enameled green, fo charmingly diverfified in its colours, and more delight-fully foft to the feet, than if covered with a carpet of filk?" Then recolle&ing the

purple

purple which ornaments the fhoulders of royalty, and too frequently conceals, under its majeftic colour, many vices ;— "Never," continued he, "did the roman emperors, in the moft fplendid habiliments, exceed this embroidery of nature."

If any tree difappointed him of its fruit, he would kindly overlook the defeft, reprefenting how neceffary it was for them to be fometimes excufed the tribute due to their mafter, to prevent their exhaufting their ftrength and fubftance. When the fruits did not arrive to ripenefs and perfeftion, he would attribute it either to his negleffing to cultivate them in proper feafon, or to his leaving more upon the trees than they were capable of nourifhing; never fuffering himfelf to arraign providence, or rafhly to condemn the innocent.

On his retiring, the trees who had lent an attentive ear to the old Gentleman's converfation, congratulated themfelves, faying to each other; "How thankful ought we to be for our good fortune, in being placed in the fervice, and under the proteffion of fo excellent a mafter, who fmiles his approbation and praifes on our good qualities, and in return for our fruit, beftows beſtows the kindeſt care and moſt flattering acknowledgments, generouſly overlooking our demerits, and laying the blame of an unſuccefsful year, to ſome neglect or omiſſion on his part."

M O R A L.

Minds, worth correcting, are more affected by a liberal indulgence to their foibles, than by the juſteſt reproaches, or the ſtrongeſt reaſoning.

XXII.

XXII. The Two Fishermen.

Virtue, industry, or abilities, cannot always secure a person from misfortune ; but the consciousness of not having deserved it, will ever give him fortitude to bow, with a dignified resignation, to the wise dispensations of providence.

FABLE.

TWO Men, who gained their livelihood by fishing, went two or three times to throw their nets together, but it was not with the same luck ; the one returning, every night, loaded with fish, while the other retired with empty panniers

niers. The unfortunate one thinking his ill fuccefs proceeded from not having chofen fo elegible a place as his companion, rofe before him that he might occupy it the firft, and throwing his net, made fure of drawing up a booty that fhould compenfate for his late fevere difappointment, but alas! all his endeavors were vain! Fate had determined otherwife, and each time he threw his net, he had the mortification to fee the fifh pafs on to his neighbour, and at night found himfelf as miferable as ever.

On a day, when the fortunate one had caught a large Pike, which the other had flattered himfelf with the hope of taking, he addreffed the Fifh, with faying "why are you more willing to enrich my companion than me?—why pafs me, and with your company, go to him in preference?" —"My friend," anfwered the Pike, "I fcarcely know how to anfwer you: but it is very certain, if I could follow my own inclination, I would rather ftop at your net, but I am irrefiftibly preffed forward by your evil genius."—"I am not poffeffed of power fufficient to conquer your evil genius," faid a gentleman paffing by, who had heard the fubject of his complaints, " but I am fo happy as to be able to change
your

your poverty into affluence ;" and immediately gave him a purfe, which compenfated for all his former mifery.

M O R A L.

It is fo much in the power of the rich to make, with a mere trifle, fo many people happy, that it fhould be among the firft principles that are inculcated in their youth.

XXIII

XXIII. The WEAZEL, the DEER, and the ELEPHANT.

Weak minds and cowardly hearts only, suffer themselves to be influenced by presages, omens, or signs ; which are the different terms given to the phantoms of ignorant brains.

F A B L E.

AN ELEPHANT, who was on the point of executing some great design, was proceeding to the place he had fixed on as a rendezvous for his troops, when he met a Deer, whose erected head, and bold spreading horns, tempted him to ask him to join him

him, in his intended enterprise. The Deer, brave in words, and courageous in theory, promised every thing the hardiest beast could undertake. While the Elephant was representing to him the honor which was to be acquired in this undertaking, a Weazel crossed the road, and instantly threw the Deer into the greatest alarm, which the Elephant endeavoured to calm, by shewing the weaknefs of feeling fear at the fight of fuch an infignificant animal : " It is not the animal I am afraid of," anfwered the Deer, "But its appearance juft at this time is a bad omen for your expedition," and endeavoured to fupport this doctrine by the affertions of many of his friends and relations, who had actually experienced the truth of it.

The Elephant ridiculed the folly of fuch prognoftics, and laughed at his timidity ; and enforcing his cenfures with great ftrength of reafoning, he prevailed on him to banifh his fears, which were a reflection on himfelf, and to keep his former refolution of following him ; but fcarcely had they proceeded an hundred fteps, before they heard the crowing of a cock in a neighbouring Village, which entirely put to flight the little courage, that the Elephant's reafonings reasonings had revived, and turning from him, he advised the Elephant to give up all thoughts of his present enterprise, for that the Cock never crowed at that hour, but that it foreboded, some very great misfortune to those who obstinately persisted in their design.

"It is," said the Elephant, "for the Lion to fear, not for you, or me; he has a natural antipathy to the sound of a Cock crowing, which shakes his noble breast with dread, but you have not that excuse; besides, do not think me so narrow-minded, so faint of heart, as to be deterred from prosecuting a glorious undertaking by every trifle cowards choose to dignify with the name of omens, to screen the dastardly timidity of their own souls; and turning his back, with contempt, upon the Deer, he joined his troops, which were by this time arrived.

The combat was soon decided in his favor: Returning loaded with riches, he passed, crowned with honors, close to the Deer's cover, who seeing the fallacy of placing faith in tokens, and sensible of the disgrace he had incurred by his cowardly desertion, hid himself among the bushes to conceal the shame he felt.

MORAL.

M O R A L.

No dependence can be placed in cowards, for they are generally boafters, and of courfe liars ;—too defpicable for fociety or fervice.

H   XXIV.

XXIV. The FIG-TREE, deftroyed by Lightning.

*Thofe who fly from their friends in adverfity,
draw down upon themfelves contempt and
hatred ; for no misfortunes, no poverty
whatever can reflect a difgrace equal to
fuch a proof of a depraved difpofition.*

FABLE.

NATURE had been fo indulgent to the
Birds of a particular country, that
fhe had not only provided them with plen-
ty of food, but had made it her ftudy to
contribute to their pleafure, as well as profit, by planting a Fig-Tree on a little Hil-
lock

lock near the borders of a clear ſtream : The beauty of the ſituation,—its vicinity to a refreſhing river,—the ſweetly pleaſant flavour of its fruit,—its ſpreading branches covered with leaves, large and thick enough to form a moſt delightful ſhade, rendered it the conſtant reſort of every kind of birds.

On the latter end of September, after a ſuffocating heat, the atmoſphere grew thick, —the ſky became clouded,—heaven low-ered, and in the moſt dreadful thunder ſpoke its anger. The birds who were en-joying themſelves on the branches of the Fig-Tree, finding, by the rain, which be-gan to penetrate their feathers, that there was every reaſon to expect a furious tem-peſt, were under the neceſſity of taking flight to the neareſt ſhelter.

Scarcely were they in ſafety before they heard the moſt tremendous claps of thun-der ; the repeated rollings of which, ſpread general terror throughout the country, but its depredations were particularly exer-ciſed on the beautiful Fig-Tree, which fell a ſacrifice to its rage, and in an inſtant were all its grateful fruits and boaſted leaves conſumed.

The

The ftorm being appeafed, and the rain-
bow appearing, as a fignal of peace being
eftablifhed in the heavens, the birds ventur-
ed from their afylum, ·flying immediately
towards their much-prized Tree : but it
being ftripped of all its honors—all its riches : poor,—forfaken, and labouring under
affliction, they no longer recollected the
friend who had afforded them an agreeable
fhade in many a fultry day ; but turning
from it, with coldnefs, affected perfect ignorance, where fo fudden and fo fevere an
alteration feemed to authorife it.

At laft it was vifited by fome Turtles and
Becafigs ; who wifhing to condole with it
on the melancholy reverfe of fortune it had
experienced, and thinking the foothing
voice of friendfhip would prove a confolation, affectionately perched, as ufual, upon
its now withered branches without being
difgufted at its appearance, or offended
with the fmell of the thunder with which
it was infected.

Some Vultures, Kites, and other birds of
prey, with all the cruelty of their barbarous
natures, expreffed their furprife at their
folly, in chufing fuch a defolated habitation,
when near them was an oak, the tempting
green

green of which, invited them to repofe themfelves under its extenfive fhade; earneftly perfuading them to fly from the Fig-Tree, by reprefenting to them that there was neither honor, pleafure, or even fafety in attaching themfelves to a Tree which Jupiter had thought deferving of fo fevere a punifhment.

" I have ever truly loved it," anfwered the Turtle;—" He has fo often nourifhed me," faid the Becafig;—" And I," continued an old Woodpidgeon, "have experienced his generofity in fo many favours, that while I have life, I will devote myfelf to it;—green, or withered;—dead, or living; fortunate, or unfortunate; I attach myfelf to it forever, determined to fhare its fate, whether good or ill."

M O R A L.

Real friendfhip is like an evergreen, which feafons cannot change; and which will grow in the pooreft, as well as in the richeft foil.

H3   XXV

XXV. The EAGLE and YOUNG RAVENS.

Virtue and courage do not always attend
upon rank, however invited by education,
courted by parents, or fought for in the
beau-monde.   They, who pay refpect to the
fummons of a really good heart only, muft
frequently condefcend to become the guefts
of the moft uninformed and leaft accom-
plifhed of the creation ; of thofe, whofe
whole merit confifts in being good fons ;
good hufbands ; good fathers, and honeft
men :—thus unfafhionable is virtue.

F A B L E.

A N EAGLE had unfortunately found,
by many years experience, that her
Children

Children degenerated from the virtues of their anceſtors, and that of all the young ones ſhe had reared, none had ever proved themſelves poſſeſſed of the generoſity of mind that her whole race had heretofore been happy enough to boaſt. She therefore formed the reſolution of procuring a Raven's eggs, and mixing them with her own, hatch them all in the ſame neſt, to try if the care and attention ſhe paid them would not be a means of correcting thoſe faults which they appear to derive from nature,

Whether it were owing to a difference of food, or whether the purity of the air in ſo elevated a ſituation, had any influence over the Ravens, we cannot determine ; but as they grew, the majeſty of their manners, and the brilliant dignity of their countenances, encouraged the moſt flattering expectations ; while the young Eagles ſeemed to feel neither pleaſure, or ambition, beyond quarrelling with each other, and even in taſte, teſtified the meanneſs of their hearts, by preferring the moſt diſguſting carrion to the freſheſt veniſon.

The Eagle thinking it now time to begin to exerciſe their wings, thought to

prove

prove if they really poffeffed the courage and generofity natural to their race, by expofing them to the rays of the fun, which, though too brilliant for common birds to look at, and too warm for them to approach, ever cherifhed and revived the King of Birds. Chufing a mild day, fhe encouraged them to leave their neft altogether, and refrefh themfelves by air and exercife.

The Old Eagle watched them narrowly, and had the mortification of feeing the Ravens with only one of the young Eagles direct their courfe with a fteady wing, and undaunted eye, ftraight towards the fun; while the others, mean of heart, depraved in foul, and narrow in mind, unable to bear the luftre of that glorious luminary, fell, e'er they had reached one half its height, lamenting in cowardly complaints, their mother's indifference to their cries, who, inftead of affording that relief they had rendered themfelves undeferving of, configned them for ever, to oblivion, denying their affinity to her: "No," faid fhe, "you are not my Children, nor will I believe myfelf fo unfortunate as to be your Mother: my Children, are by nature generous, brave, and noble; you, whom I
leave

leave, to Fate, are mean, cowardly and
felfifh.

M O R A L.

Many calamities are frequently owing to
parents' configning to another, the care of
forming the hearts of their children. Education
may improve natural abilities, and good company form the manners ; but to a parent belongs
the tafk of fowing, on the firft dawn of reafon,
the feeds of virtue, and of bending the mind,
ere it has power to adopt an opinion, to receive
its inftigations.   Thus will the weeds of ill be,
choaked,—the mother be bleffed,—and fociety
adorned.

XXVI

XXVI. The Spanish Horse, and the Sumpter Horse.

In all employments of consequence, capacity, accomplishment, and knowledge, should be attended to, and should decide your choice, not birth, private worth, or long services; they have their merits, and they have also, their suitable distinctions.

F A B L E.

A Gentleman, who had held a distinguished rank, as a military man, was every year obliged to attend his duty in the army, and on that occasion generally mounted a Spanish Charger, very highly dressed for that purpose, and who for

many

many years had gained him great credit, by his obedience, activity, and spirited exertions in the field. Having received a summons from his sovereign, he mounted his favorite, ordering his groom, as usual, to saddle for himself and baggage, the Sumpter Horse, who, at first, made some resistance, but seeing his master coming unexpectedly he quietly submitted to be saddled.

The next day, on being led out of the stables, he suddenly attacked the groom, making use of his heels with a violence that astonished him; but being asked the cause, he declared he would no longer condescend to carry the baggage;—he had already submitted too long to such a degradation, and that his master took an ungenerous advantage of his patience. The groom almost frightened at the obstinacy he testified, immediately informed his master of the cause that kept him waiting, who directly went to the Sumpter Horse, and accosting him with great good nature, desired to be informed, what had thus irritated him.

"Is it not shameful,—is it not ungrateful of you," answered the Horse, "after ten years faithful service, to load me with your baggage

baggage, and that your favorite there, (I mean your Spanish Charger) who has scarcely served you three years, should be raised to all the dignity and honor of bearing on his back your noble person ?——— Mount me in turn ; let him carry the baggage, and in the diftinction of being rode by you, let me receive the reward of ten years servitude."

The mafter, who was by no means infenfible to his worth, and who efteemed his fidelity too much to mortify him ; with great goodnefs, endeavoured to make him admit the reafons which had actuated him: " You have," faid he, "too rough a pace ; you have not had the advantages of educution, to fit you for the manœuvers of the field, which require great fupplenefs and activity, and a quick and implicit obedience to the moft unexpected command ; to which, unaccuftomed to the hurry and confufion of a battle, you would be unequal. On the other hand, my war Horfe though not fuperior to you in intrinfic merit, is ftill fo in abilities for the bufinefs I employ him on, and would be very incapable of undertaking your bufinefs, from the finenefs of his make, which is too weak in the loins to carry both my groom and my baggage, which muft convince you,

that

that if I liftened to your requeft, I fhould be the caufe, not only of the death of my beautiful Charger, but of your's and mine alfo : I am well convinced of your merits ; —they fuit the line I have placed you in ; —every care is taken of you, and I am perfuaded bad advice has actuated you to rebel againft my commands ; but I forgive you ; beware for the future, and difcover the inftigator of your difobedience."

The Horfe touched with the generofity of his mafter, and the mildnefs with which he endeavoured to remove, inftead of refenting his difcontent, acknowledged his fault, and owned that he was mifled by the bad advice of a Mule who was his neighbour in the ftables : At thefe words he quietly turned to be faddled, and the mafter ordered the Mule to be chaftifed, and deprived of half his general allowance of corn.

M O R A L.

Thus mifled by bad advice, and prefumptuoufly confident in their own abilities, people too frequently lofe an eligible fituation by afpiring to one they are unequal to fill, either with juftice, or propriety ; and thus become a detriment to fociety, of which, had they liftened to prudence and moderation, they might have been ufeful members.

XXVII

XXVII. The HORSE with the NICKED TAIL, and the ASSES.

Fashion should not be allowed to gain so great an ascendency, as to render a person the subject of ridicule ; a respect to the customs of the world shews sense ; the vanity, that leads to particularity, testifies folly.

FABLE.

A FINE HUNTER, from which a youth had just dismounted, got loose, still bearing on his back, all the gaudy trappings of ton, and no less vain of his gay caparisons, than pleased with his liberty,

paraded

paraded about with great pride and satisfact-
ion, carrying a high head to all whom he
happened to meet in his momentary escape
from slavery; among the number, chance
threw in his way, were two Asses, who
returning from market, were unadorned
even by rich merchandise, having nothing
on their backs but empty bags, which served them both as a saddle and as an ornament.

As soon as the Hunter discovered them
thus equiped, he neither could nor wished
to conceal his mirth and contempt, but
bursting into a fit of laughter, enjoyed the
vulgarity of their appearance, which was
again repeated when he perceived their
long ungainly tails, uncombed, clogged
with dirt, and matted with straw:—" Pray"
said he, "what is your business, and what
your disposition?—Do you carry those tails
as an ornament; or to render a public service, by sweeping the roads?—And what
is your reason for bearing on your backs,
those coarse, homely sacks?——" In these
sacks," replied they, "we have carried the
support of the kingdom; the bringing them
back empty, we look upon both as a relief
and an honor; thinking ourselves distinguished in doing an essential service to the
state

ftate, and think ourfelves truly happy, and amply rewarded, in being permitted to re-pofe the remainder of the day, and imme-diately turned out, on our return home, to feaft on thiftles and thofe herbs nature has taught us to efteem luxurious."

"Poor wretches!" replied the Spanifh Courfer, "how low your ideas!—How ri-diculous your wifhes!—How contemptible your fentiments!—Truely beneath my no-tice!" Saying which, he began capering, to fhew off his figure and his agility, and to make them envy the fuperiority of his trap-pings, and wonder at his proficiency in grace and elegance, which requiring great exertion, and the fun beginning to grow powerful, he found all the inconvenience of that faddle he had fo much prided him-felf upon, and which had given him, in his own ideas, fuch a diftinction; but when, with the heat of the fun, the Flies began to fwarm and attack him, he fenfibly found himfelf at a lofs for that defence, which the tails of thofe he had ridiculed afforded them; and truely did he regret they had made him fo fafhionable, at the expence of the greateft comfort that could be experi-enced.

The

The Affes, feeing him fretting and impatient, flying here and there, as if the greateft misfortune in the world had happened to him ; after amufing themfelves in their turn with the diftrefs which his vanity deferved, could not refift expreffing to him the fuperior comforts, of which, notwithftanding all his boaft, they efteemed themfelves poffeffed.

" Thanks to the Gods!" cried they, "if we are lefs adorned, we are at leaft exempt from all the inconveniencies annexed to greatnefs and high diftinctions ; and we have learnt (from your folly, prefumption, and ungratified pride) that conforming to the rules of nature,—enjoying her gifts, and checking every afpiring wifh, is the road to happinefs."

M O R A L.

Senfe, beauty, and accomplifhments, fhould be confidered as the three attendant graces of virtue ; but never fhould be efteemed her fupport, or be fuffered to impofe on the mind as her reprefentatives.

I   XXVIII

XXVIII. The Ostrich, and Bird of Paradise.

No connection can long subsist between two persons of different dispositions and sentiments : To avoid all intimacy; to decline all intercourse, is the most prudent plan to prevent enmity, and preserve good neighbourhood.

FABLE.

AN Ostrich having satisfied his rapacious appetite, amused himself with loitering about the country : In his ramble, having his head elevated on high, he perceived a remarkable Bird, whose figure and plumage

plumage he was perfectly unacquainted with, and being curious to difcover from whence he came, he remained fixed for fome time in obferving him, hoping to fee him perch upon fome tree, that he might more fteadily take a view of him : He was kept in expectation a long while, but ftill impatiently watched, thinking every moment that he might find it neceffary to reft after the fatigue of, what he thought, an incredible long flight; but finding that he maintained it with equal facility, he attributed it to the vanity of appearing to poffefs fuperior ftrength and breath to the generality of birds.

The Bird ftill kept itfelf on the wing, flying as inclination led, till the Oftrich, out of all temper at being thus kept in fufpence, addreffed him, inviting him to earth, and requefting him to refrefh himfelf by a few minutes repofe. The bird replying, that the earth was not his element, but that nature had given him the air for his habitation, the Oftrich anfwered, he fhould remain as fhort a time on earth as he thought proper, but entreated to be indulged with the fatisfaction of converfing with him a little. "I am not defpicable," faid he, "as you may perceive by the majefty and

noblenefs

noblenefs of my figure, and the value of my feathers."

"However beautiful they may be," faid the bird, "I know they do not poffefs the power of raifing that grofs, clumfy body of your's :—Remain where you are ; all communication between us is incompatible with our natures :—Know that I am the Bird of Paradife, who have no legs to vifit the earth ; and your wings are too weak, tho' to appearance, ungracefully ftrong, to waft you into the air ; befides your food confifts of the groffeft and moft terreftial quality, while celeftial dew forms all my repaft."

MORAL.

The worldly-minded man, blind to the future, places all his hopes and fears in the tranfient events of this life. The philofopher, ere it is too late, withdraws himfelf from its vanities, and trufting for happinefs and reward above, offers the fulfilling the duties of his ftarion to the utmoft of his abilities, as an humble plea for mercy.

XXIX

XXIX. Two Colts, and their Dams.

To reproach a child with its ignorance, is exposing your own shame, and incurring the censure of the wise for neglecting an education, which it is the peculiar duty of parents to superintend themselves.

FABLE.

TWO beautiful Mares, distinguished by birth and merit, as superior to any in the country, brought forth two Foals at the same time: from whom, trusting to the fame of their genealogy, they entertained the highest expectations. They had scarcely reckoned two months, when they

I3   began

began to form plans for educating them in a manner fuitable to their rank and future employment. One of them immediately hired a groom to attend her Foal, and to inftruct him, according to his ftrength, bringing him by degrees, from gentle exercife, to acquire vigour equal to diftinguifh himfelf in the race; to bear off the prize at the ring, and to obtain honor in in the field.

The other Mare paffing by, during a courfe her friend's Foal was practifing, and feeing him, though fweating very profufely, preffed forward and urged to ftill greater exertions, cried out with anger, "How inhuman!—Poffeffed of one child only, and fuffer it, when fcarcely able to walk, to be tortured into a variety of poftures, and trained to feats beyond its ftrength!—Not thus fevere am I to my child; contenting myfelf, during its youth, with having it taught to walk with grace."

Some time after, the groom endeavouring to make the fame Colt curvett, and trying to train him to the Manage, (the manœuvers of which he rapidly acquired,) this foolifh Mare could not refrain from quarrelling with her friend, declaring fhe
acted

acted more like a jealous ftep-mother to-wards her Colt, than a mother affectionate-ly attached : At the fame time fhe ordered *her* Son to be brought out, who attracted general admiration : his mane, of the moft' brilliant whitenefs, trained on the ground ; his tail waved with elegance, and his trap-pings were, to the laft degree, magnificent. With this beautiful exterior, he bore all the appearance of an animated fpirit, and an unrivalled vigor.

The approbation he met with, determin-ed his Dam to prefent him, in the fame ca-parifons, at a tournament; where, as be-fore, his beauty drew all eyes upon him, none doubting but that his fuccefs would equal the expectations his appearance cre-ated. The effect does not always anfwer the attempt, for fcarcely did he fuffer the groom to mount, before he threw him to the ground; and while his companion was gain-ing univerfal applaufe from the various ex-ercifes which he performed with grace and eafe, this ufelefs beauty gave his Mother's folly its reward, by kicking her each time fhe exhorted him to endeavor to gain fome degree of praife, and to reflect fome little honor upon Her. He reproached her for the difgrace her foolifh fondnefs had drawn

I4   npon

upon him, fince it was impoffible for him
to perform more than he had been taught;
which, from her weaknefs, had been mere-
ly to walk with grace, and carry his head
with dignity.

M O R A L.

An amiable and affectionate Parent cannot
feel a ftronger motive to exert the moft zealous
attention in the education of her Child, during
his infancy, than the hope of being rewarded
by feeing him enjoy honor and happinefs in
manhood :—For thofe who are infenfible to fo
animated a pleafure, and whofe felfifhnefs will
not fuffer them to look beyond their own gratification, it is neceffary to reprefent the education of a Child in a different light—to endeavor to convince them, that it is a ftrict duty impofed on them by the Almighty ;—that it is a
debt due to fociety,—and a refpect to which the
memory of our anceftors has a claim ; to
whofe virtues, we cannot pay a greater defer-
ence, than by endeavoring to make them live
again in their pofterity.

XXX

XXX. The LION and MONKEY.

A wise Prince can never suppose himself so free from foibles, and so superior to his Subjects, as to believe every action of his life safe from the shafts of ridicule.

FABLE.

A LION, who was subject to give way to the most violent passions on the slightest provocations and who, from such repeated furies, kept his kingdom in continual dread, had nearly, by indulging this fault, forfeited his life to his exasperated subjects.

A

A Fox had obferved, that when his anger was created, by lafhing his tail, he irritated himfelf to a degree of madnefs, and that till he did fo, his temper was, in comparifon, quite mild ; he therefore affembled a party of animals, to whom he communicated the obfervation he had made, propofing at the fame time, that a method to prevent fuch frequent returns of rage fhould be deliberated upon. Some few propofed murdering him ; but the majority were too loyal to admit that idea for a moment : Others thought the cutting off his tail would be the beft plan, fince he appeared to make ufe of it for the purpofe of raifing his choler to a higher pitch than the offence deferved; and that perhaps when deprived of that ftimulus, he might become much lefs able to terrify his inferiors with thofe tremendous burfts of paffion, they had fo frequently experienced : Every one commended this refolution ; but who was to undertake it ?—Silence prevailed,—not one offered to brave fo great a danger ; and with great regret they were obliged to reject that fcheme.

However another was fuggefted by the Monkey, that promifed to have all the effect, without the danger attending the latter
ter

ter; which was, with the affiftance of
the Dormoufe, getting the Lion to fleep,
and during his flumber, he would tie his
tail on his back, fo firmly, that his not being able, in his rage to loofen it, might
prove the means of correcting his errors,
without their running any rifk in their own
perfons, or injuring the facred one of their
King.

The affembly greatly applauded the in-
vention, which was executed fo cleverly,
and with fo much dexterity, that the Lion
did not awake till fome time after it was ac-
complifhed; but when he did, as was expected, he was very highly offended at feeing himfelf furrounded by animals who appeared ridiculing him, and he determined inftantly to chaftife them for their infolence;
but finding himfelf prevented from making
ufe of his tail, he prudently confidered that
he fhould, by fhewing refentment, only en-
creafe the ridiculous light in which they
now beheld him; therefore fubduing his
defire of vengeance, he treated the circum-
ftance as a frolick, and joined in the laugh
againft himfelf.

M O R A L.

M O R A L.

A Prince is more culpable in indulging to an impetuofity of difpofition than a private perfon, whofe power not being very extenfive, the fault brings the punifhment with it; but un-bridled paffion in a Sovereign, too frequently facrifices, as victims to his impatience, the moft deferving, perhaps the moft faithful, of his fub-jects.

XXXI

XXXI. The LAMB crowned with Flowers.

It requires a liberal mind,—a generous heart, —and a good understanding, to bear a sudden rise of fortune with moderation and affability

FABLE.

A SHEPHERD singled out from his flock a beautiful Lamb, on whom he fixed all his affections, feeding him from his own hands—suffering him to drink out of his own cup,—providing him with shelter from the rigor of winter, and forming, in summer, a cool arbour of the sweetest shrubs, as a retreat from the scorching rays of the sun.

The

The reft of the flock, from fo great a diftinction, began to think themfelves flighted, and had it in contemplation to make their complaints to the Shepherd, but were prevented by one of the old ones, who reprefented to them, that notwithftanding the great partiality fhewn to the favored Lamb, yet they could not, with any juftice, accufe their mafter of inattention to them. "Did he not," faid an old Ewe, "watch over us day and night, to protect us from the wolf?—Does he not carefully fearch for the beft pafture to fupply us with food? —and is he not anxioufly folicitous to preferve our health; to which he pays daily attention ?"

Such ftrength of reafoning they could not confute ; they therefore filenced their murmurs, and paying refpect to the advice of their wife parent, refolved, for the fake of their mafter and benefactor, to carefs that Lamb which had lately created their envy and jealoufy ; and by that means engage the Shepherd to be more impartial in his careffes.

This good intention they practifed, till the Shepherd growing attached, even to idolatry, began to decorate his wool with
bows

bows of ribbon, and braids of filken cords. No longer able to bear fo confpicuous a proof of diftinction, all their former hatred revived with redoubled inveteracy, and giving themfelves up to the gratification of their difguft, they entered into an agree- ment among themfelves, of banifhing him from their fociety, and flying from him wherever he appeared, except when they were obliged, from the immediate prefence of their mafter, to affociate with him.

The Shepherd, who thought he could not be too lavifh towards one fo much be- loved, and centering in him all his happi- nefs and all his amufement, was conftantly inventing fome new ornament to teftify his regard : Amongft thofe which his foolifh fondnefs induced him to prefent the Lamb with, were baubles for the ears, to which he tied them with ribbon : This complet- ed a vanity his fenfe was by no means proof againft, and encouraged him to re- queft that he might have his horns gilt, and his head crowned with flowers. No foon- er was he thus adorned, than the flock im- mediately prepared to quit their fervice, and the Shepherd himfelf, who had been hitherto blind to his follies, and had devot- ed to him every fentiment of affection and
every

every act of tendernefs, now opened his eyes, and regarding him with the cool impartiality of reafon, found his new acquired ornaments had rendered him fo deformed and reprefented his vanity, folly, and infolence, in fuch a confpicuous light ; that his love inftantly changed into hatred, and no longer able to endure the fight of him, he forbad him ever to appear again in his prefence.

M O R A L.

Thofe who chufe their friends merely from perfonal advantages, will draw from the world an imputation on their underftanding, and meet, in a difappointment, the punifhment due to their folly.

XXXII

XXXII. The Stag and Wounded Doe.

Pleafure, or engagements will, by a good Chriftian and a humane heart, be readily facrificed to the fuperior gratification of affifting a fellow-creature in diftrefs.

F A B L E.

A Stag who had given his word that he would attend a great feaft, to which a number of animals were invited, as well for pleafure, as on public bufinefs; being detained till very late by fome private affairs of his own, took a fhort road that he might make up for the delay, and as he was fwiftly purfuing his courfe, he heard,

K

from

from behind a bush, the cries of diftrefs; ftopping a moment, he liftened attentively, and approaching the place from whence he thought the founds iffued, he foon difco-vered a Doe pierced with an arrow, and dying for want of affiftance.

"Poor beaft," faid the Stag!—"Is that the only wound of which you complain?" "Yes," replied the Doe, "in this wound confifts the whole caufe of my grief; the iron, which remains in the flefh, will foon occafion my death," "Comfort yourfelf," faid the Stag, "I fhall foon have the plea-fure of curing you, if you have courage to permit me to try, I know of an infallible medicine, though you imagine yourfelf paffed hopes."

He then expatiated on the virtues of the Dittany, which had the power of drawing out the iron by opening the wound; and accurately defcribing both the herb, and the part of the country where it was to be found, recommended her to go imme-diately in fearch of it, and apply it to the part affected: Thus inftructed, the poor Doe, made a vain attempt to practife this advice, but the excrutiating pain, and lofs of blood fhe had fuffered, rendered her perfectly

ly unequal, even to the change of her place, which being obferved by the Stag, it drove from his memory, feaft, company, pleafure, and bufinefs; interefted only for the life of a fellow-creature, he flew himfelf in fearch of this valuable herb, and returning with the utmoft expedition, applied it to her fide, where in a fhort time, the iron, as if drawn by great force, flew out of the wound, leaving the Doe almoft overcome with gratitude and joy.

After thanking the Stag very affectionately, and attempting to exprefs the fenfe fhe entertained of fo important a fervice, finding the pain very much abated, fhe returned flowly home, bleffing the Stag; while he, no lefs gratified, felt highly rewarded for the trifling facrifice of an agreeable engagement.

M O R A L.

Sovereigns fhould not efteem themfelves exempt from giving, even perfonal affiftance, and fulfilling that claim which one chriftian has a right to expect from another; however mean of birth the one, and elevated in rank is the other whofe attention is required.

XXXIII, The GENTLEMAN, and the HARES and RABBITS.

Prejudiced by names which bear authority,
little-minded people are awed into terror
by the presence of kings, magistrates, and
superiors, fancying them like beasts of prey:
To remove such prejudices among the vul-
gar, and to give them confidence, is the
duty of a sovereign and his servants; to
effect which, a king should often gratify
his people with his presence, and receive
them with a dignity tempered by mildness,
that shall court their affection, and remove
their fears, without lessening their respect;
he should also make choice of such magis-
trates, as will, by proving themselves pro-
tectors

tectors of their peace, convince his people
that their king watches, like a tender father, over their rights and priveleges ;
then will the names of the great be menti-
oned with pleafure and refpect, inftead of
fear and difguft.

F A B L E.

WHETHER a tyger, a bear, or a
lion, had made their appearance,
with hoftile intent in the country ; or that
a general terror had fuddenly taken poffeffion of the hearts of the animals, naturally timid, is the moft certain way of ac-
counting for the panic, which fpread all
over the foreft, was never decided ; but
fuch was the fear of fome impending danger, that Hares, Rabbits, Deer, &c. dared
not venture to leave their coverts ; and
what encreafed their fright was, that fome,
as is generally the cafe, liftening only to
the dictates of fear, imagined fome dreadful cataftrophe, and reported as true, that
there was a monftrous beaft arrived in the
foreft, without particularifing its form,
which depopulated all the country, laying
it wafte wherever it was fure of not meeting with refiftance, and added to injuftice,
the moft unheard-of cruelty ; not contented with murdering whomever he met with,
3K   but

but afterwards fucking their blood, and throwing their carcaffes into the lay-ftalls, as a fhock to friends and relations who might unfortunately fee them.

As thefe terror-ftruck little animals were affembled to form fome plan to fave themfelves from the ruin with which they were threatened, a. young Gentleman appeared all of a. fudden, mounted on a managed Horfe of Spain, who amufed himfelf with making him paffage. A Rabbit was the firft who difcovered him, and taking him for a Centaur, immediately gave the alarm, imagining it to be the. dreadful Monfter that had been predicted ; at the fame time flied to give warning of the approach of their furious enemy, which was fo rapidly communicated to all parties, that none doubted the truth of the former report : but all concealed themfelves under the firft fhelter they could meet with.

While they were all fuffering under the moft painful fufpence, as a. Deer and a few Rabbits were hid behind fome bufhes near the fuppofed Monfter, they had an opportunity of obferving him: He ftill continued amufing himfelf with exercifing his horfe through the manœuvers of the

Manage

Manage, now Curvetting, now Piafering;
then Paffaging right and left, vaulting, re-
treating, advancing; all with a grace, eafe,
and compofure that evidently proved his
defign was amufement, not hoftility, which
encouraged them to leave their coverts and
advance to take a nearer view of this
ftrange Phænomenon ; when they were
furprifed at the beauty of his face,—the
amiable expreffion of his countenance,—
the grace and dignity of his form and manners, more deferving of the higheft admiration; more likely to create love and adora-
tion, than horror and hatred ; and gaining
courage from the mildnefs and benignity
of his afpect, they could not contain their
admiration ; but calling their companions,
condemned their own folly & pufillanimous
timidity, in making as an object of dread,
an animal, the foft majefty of whofe figure
entitled him to be efteemed a Deity by the
whole foreft.

M O R A L.

This fable admitting of two conftructions,
in order to render it more inftructive to young
minds, the affinity of the two morals is waved;
to explain here, the additional light in which
the fable may be viewed.—Where ever reafon
is exerted, the vapour which fear has thrown

over an object, will, of courfe, foon evaporate;
by teaching, (or rather accuftoming) children
early in life to decide by the medium of their
judgment, they will acquire coolnefs and refolution to inveftigate the caufe of a momentary
fear. inftead of blindly fubmitting themfelves
to the powerful influence of fuperftition, the
invader of peace and happinefs, and the rival
of wifdom ; the feeds of which are fcarcely,
even in this informed age, rooted out, tho' it
is proved to be the bane of fociety.

XXXIV

XXXIV. The Shepherd, Shepherd-ess, and Worms.

Live a good life, and rob death of its ter-rors :—Live well, and death will be mere-ly a tranfition from fublunary pleafures to certain and endlefs happinefs.

FABLE.

A Shepherd and Shepherdefs, who had for fome time experienced all the happinefs refulting from reciprocal and un-abating love, were fuddenly parted forever by that remorfelefs tyrant, death, who vi-fited the Shepherdefs as fhe lay afleep on a bank, under the form of a ferpent, from whofe fting fhe expired, leaving her belov-ed Shepherd inconfolable for her lofs.

He

He, after paying the tribute of unavailing tears, determined to give a more folid proof of his regret, by erecting a little monument to his ever-beloved, ever-lamented Amaranthus, which he vifited every day, carrying with him the various flowers of the feafon, to deck her tomb; added to that attention, he made it a duty to keep it perfectly clean, preventing every kind of animal from approaching it, fearful of its being contaminated with their filth.

One day, as he was, according to cuftom, hanging over the wreck of all his happinefs, and deftroying with his crook, the worms which came out of the coffin, he heard fomething like the voice of difcontent; and lending an attentive ear, he heard one, which he had juft bruifed, pronounce thefe words: "Miferable Shepherd, do not act thus cruelly to Amaranthus, once fo tenderly beloved: The worms which you crufh, thinking you do me fervice, are, in fact, a part of myfelf; and if you have difficulty in believeng me, remove the ftone which covers me."

The Shepherd had no fooner lifted it up, than he faw innumerable worms come out, and disfigure the once lovely face of his

Amaranthus

Amaranthus; addreffing him very diftinctly in thefe words: "Refpect my memory,
—cherifh a love for my virtues; but forget the form I once was: remembering, at
the fame time, that Thyrfis will one day
be what Amaranthus is now." Thefe laft
words funk fo deep into his mind, added
to the unalleviated affliction at his lofs, that
neglecting his flock, he gave up every
thought and hope to that of joining his
Amaranthus.

M O R A L.

Vanity, pride, and rivalfhip would ceafe to
prevail, did the encouragers of thofe paffions
meditate over the filent tomb: But youth has
its errors, and claims its excufes; age alone
deferves feverity and contempt, which turning
from its approaching doom, thinks to cheat time
and death, by aping the follies, without dif-
playing the generous virtue of youth; difgracing grey hairs, and difgufting Society.

XXXV

XXXV. The Aged Horse, and the Lame One,

That being surely has a claim both upon our protection and our tenderness, to whom we have unfortunately (though perhaps unintentionally) occasioned pain or grief: how depraved then must the heart be, which, deaf to the calls of humanity, insults the person he has injured, and treats with contempt, one with whose misery he has to reproach himself: Such characters, to the disgrace of human nature, do exist:—Go thou, and do otherwise.

FABLE.

A

A Remarkable fine Horfe, but unfortunately fo extremely lame in one leg, as to be paffed all hope of cure, was conducting to a lay-ftall, by a rough unfeeling groom, when he met an old fpanifh Horfe, with whom, in more profperous days, when was he efteemed an ornament to the army, he had been very intimate. The Spanifh Horfe immediately recollected his old acquaintance, and ftruck with his dejected countenance, tenderly enquired the caufe of his affliction.

To which the other anfwered: "You are well acquainted with the great and important fervices I have rendered my mafter, by procuring him victory in every tournament, pleafure in the chace, and honor in the field of battle. Two months fince, we ran a Stag, in which exercife he continued me beyond my ftrength, but knowing his eagernefs in the chace, and his impetuofity of temper, I had not the courage to complain, but perfevered in the purfuit, till perfectly exhaufted, and overcome with fatigue, I fell, in endeavoring to leap a ditch, and broke my leg.

I had not been at home a fortnight before my mafter, at the inftigation of this cruel

cruel groom, whofe avarice wifhed to facrifice me for the profit of my fkin, ordered him to lead me to the lay-ftall, forget-
ting in one moment, years of faithful fervices and zealous friendfhip, in contributing
both to his honor, glory, and happinefs.

The big tear of compaffion rolled
down the generous face of the Spanifh
Steed, while he liftened to his friend's af-
fecting complaints, and he deeply regretted he could not enfure to his diftreffed acquaintance the good fortune fate had allot-
ted himfelf; "for though," faid he, "it is no
longer in my power to render him, even
half thofe fervices, which in my beft days,
were inadequate to his goodnefs, yet this
generous mafter pitying my infirmities, en-
deavours to foften the feverity with which
old age advances, enabling me, in fome
meafure, to combat its rigour, by the tendereft attention to my health, feeding me
with the fame liberality, as when I was
equal to earning my food ; and having me
carefully bathed, and conftantly attended
every day : Nor does he confine his atten-
tions to the prefervation of my life alone,
but by his flattering praifes on the abilities
of my youth, his kind careffes, and the
entertainment of being, when the weather
is

is fine, thus led out to enjoy the air, he leaves my grateful heart without a wifh ungratified.

Scarcely had he time to finifh thofe laft words, when the inhuman groom tired with waiting fo long, forced, with fevere blows, his victim to proceed about a hundred fteps, where, to the grief of the Spanifh Horfe, he faw his old friend murdered and flayed.

M O R A L,

There are few who efteem a domeftic after they have loft the power of ferving them ; and there are ftill fewer who love a friend when he no longer gratifies their felf-love.

XXXVI.

XXXVI. Of Armed Animals.

*The firſt idea that ſhould be inculcated in a
ſoldier, is, that all depends upon his courage; for an army may reſt its hopes of ſucceſs more upon the unanimity of the offi-
cers, and the courage, intrepid coolneſs,
and implicit obedience of the ſoldiers; than
on the force of numbers; which proves
how neceſſary it is for a good general to
be a diſciplinarian.*

FABLE.

A Leopard, grown proud of the character of bravery, which a lucky con-
queſt

queft acquired him, thought to add to his confequence, by giving defiance to his King, and arrogantly ufurping, by force of arms, a part of the country which was particularly appropriated, by the Lion, to his own ufe.

He was feconded, as is generally the cafe, by thofe, who, either miftaking their own intereft, wifhed to gratify a rebellious fpirit ; or, being idle, made the doing of milchief (the natural confequence of idlenefs) both an employment and a pleafure. The Leopard's army confifted of all the malecontents of the foreft, which amounting to a vaft number, gave him the moft fanguine hopes of fuccefs ; but the Lion, more wife, and better experienced, determined to avail himfelf of a dear-bought leffon, which the lofs of a late battle had taught him, and recollecting that his former ill fuccefs proceeded from recruiting none but thofe who poffeffed weapons of offence alone, refolved to admit thofe only, who could boaft of defenfive ones alfo.

According to this refolution he affembled thofe of his fubjects on whom he could depend, chufing from the numbers which flocked to his ftandard, the Rhinoceros,

defended by an impenetrable fhield of
fcales,—the Crocodile,—the Hedge-Hog—
Porcupine, and Tortoife, no lefs fortified
for defence; befides innumerable other
animals, on whom nature had beftowed an
armour for protection againft the attacks of
their Enemies.

Thus fupported, the Lion, fearlefs of
the fuperiority of numbers, undauntedly
met his antagonift, and after bravely fuf-
taining the violence of the firft onfet of fo
powerful an army, his well-difciplined,
well-defended troops, foon turned the fate
of the battle; for fuffering his adverfaries
to exhauft their ftrength and fpirit, while
they themfelves acted only upon the defenfive, he watched the time, when the army
of the Leopard, elated with the hopes of
having daunted his forces,—deaf to the
voice of command,—and trufting to their
own fkill, would lay themfelves open to a
defeat.

This foon happened, and the Lion as
quickly made his advantage of it; for he
attacked them with a fury which the coolnefs
and firmnefs that his troops had at firft expreffed, and which his enemies had miftaken
for cowardice, rendered fo perfectly unexpected;

pected; that it inftantly occafioned the confufion of the Leopard's army, which immediately taking flight was warmly purfued,
and entirely banifhed the foreft; and the
victorious troops, enriched with the fpoils
of the conquered party, returned home in
triumph.

M O R A L.

A good caufe infpires troops with confidence :
it is, therefore, the duty of a general to render
himfelf beloved, by friendly acts, and a liberal
attention to his foldiers ;—to render himfelf
feared, by the ftrictnefs of his difcipline, and
to make himfelf chearfully obeyed, by conforming to that difcipline himfelf : Thus will
foldiers follow their leader, in the perfuafion
that the caufe he efpoufes muft be right, and
that under fuch a commander fuccefs awaits
them.

XXXVII.

XXXVII. The Hawk and Peacock.

*A false friend, indifferent to your welfare,
—an enemy to your interest, and attentive
only to his own, feels no compunction in
adding treachery to deceit, by enriching
himself at your expence.*

FABLE.

A Hawk having frequently admired
the rich plumes which adorned the
tail of the Peacock, contracted a friend-
ship with that bird, hoping to turn the affluence of his dress to some account. His
warm professions of friendship and appa-
rently sincere assurances of esteem, caused
the

the Peacock to admit this fycophant to all that unreferve and familiarity allowed to long-chofen friends.

About the beginning of that feafon when birds drop their feathers, the Hawk chofe to exert the influence he had acquired, by flattery and fervility, over his new friend ; and going to him early one morning, earneftly, but very refpectfully, requefted him to give him a few of thofe feathers which were no longer of ufe to him, that he might appear with more dignity at a wedding to which he was going. The Peacock efteeming the requeft as a compliment paid to his extraordinary beauty, prefented them to the Hawk with all the grace of fatisfied vanity.

Two days after, the Hawk again called on his friend for the fame purpofe, and was as liberally treated. In the evening he returned in hafte, and with great eagernefs, entreated to have a few more of thofe which were not loofe. The Peacock felt furprifed and offended, but not knowing what prefling occafion might render him fo urgent, he concealed his indignation, and generoufly fhook his tail feveral times, to fupply the avarice of his friend.

L3　　　　　Two

Two Pidgeons, who faw the tranfaftion, were charmed with the generofity teftified by the Peacock, and no lefs fenfible than the Hawk, of his beauty, they could not refift the temptation of begging a few of thofe feathers which graced his head, and formed his elegant creft: As they dropped, he prefented them with pleafure: the Pidgeons received them with gratitude, and wore them as a teftimony of their refpeft for the doner.

At this time the Hawk returned, and, feeling he could not renew his petition with propriety but ftill wifhing for more, threw off the mafk, and gravely told the Peacock, that unlefs he gave him thofe plumes which ftill remained, his former gifts would be too ufelefs to deferve, even his thanks, much lefs entitle him to his friendfhip.

The Peacock, depending upon the Hawk's regard, thought he could not give a more weighty reafon to his dear friend, for refufing him, than by defcribing the bodily pain which the obliging him would create; but the Hawk, cruel by nature, —devoid of pity, and incapable of feeling remorfe at facrificing friends, foes, or relations, to gratify himfelf, no longer condefcended

defcended to entreat, but in great anger
threw himfelf npon the Peacock, tearing
them from him with violence, regardlefs
of the wounds his powerful beak inflicted ;
and this he did with fuch fury, that it was
with the utmoft difficulty the peacock e-
fcaped from him.

Juft were his reproaches on his ingratitude :—"Obferve, falfe friend!—defpicable
fycophant ! thofe two Pidgeons," faid he,
" who efteem themfelves, for a few trifling
feathers, under fo great an obligation ;
while you, for whom I have ftript myfelf,
and to whofe requeft I never faid nay, till
no longer able to grant it, deny the friendfhip you have experienced, and rob your
benefactor of all he poffeffes ! May the
Gods revenge my caufe !—Your ingratitude is too great for my power to punifh,
—yourfelf too worthlefs for my pride to
refent ;—exemplary fhould be your chaftife-
ment !

M O R A L.

Interefted perfons are incapable of friendfhip ; felf-love, vanity, and avarice occupying
their whole foul, leave every avenue guarded
againft the entrance of fo generous a fentiment
—fo noble a virtue as friendfhip.

XXXVIII. The OLD DOG and the LION.

So feldom is it the good fortune of a Prince
to meet with Servants zealoufly attached,
as much to his honor and happinefs as a
Man, as they feel indulgent to his foibles
as a Prince, that fuch Servants fhould not
be removed on the reprefentation of others.

F A B L E.

A LION, who had ruled for many years
with all the fame due to juftice, clemency and prudence, finding himfelf approaching towards his end, more from
animated exertions for the welfare of his
ftate than from age, ordered the fon he intended

tended to leave as his fucceſſor, to be brought into his preſence, that he might, by ſalutary advice on his future conduct, fulfil the only duty that, now, remained unperformed.

He particularly urged an implicit obedience to his advice in two material points, which would enſure peace to his kingdom, and happineſs to himſelf: one of which was; never to undertake any affairs of conſequence, or hazard any enterpriſe, without firſt conſulting his mother, whoſe wiſdom and experience would prove an unerring guide: The ſecond, to continue in office thoſe old ſervants in whoſe long-tried faith he would find the beſt ſecurity, and whoſe abilities, courage and diligence, had gained them both applauſe and diſtinction in his own reign: He therefore made no doubt the young Lion would, by paying reſpect to their counſels, and honoring their virtues, ſtrengthen the kingdom ; for faithful ſubjects muſt ever be eſteemed the pillars of the ſtate.

Scarcely had the old Lion paid the debt of nature, than a tyger, a bear, and a fox, that had, for ſome time paſt, been the inveterate enemies of a large Dog, who was appointed

appointed guard to the royal cavern, whif-
pered into the young King's ear, fufpicions of this aged fervant; at the fame time
recommending him to make choice of a
younger guard, whofe ftrength and vigor
would render him a better defence than
the other's very advanced age, could
poffibly admit : befides, he was, from the
too great indulgence of his late mafter,
(who was blindly partial) grown fo extremely uncertain in his temper, that fometimes
he would carefs, and the very next moment teftify the utmoft fury at thofe who
approached the cave : Added to which, his
back was covered with the rewards of his
frequent clamours ; not to mention among
his innumerable faults, the difturbance and
nuifance he was to the neighbourhood.

The young Lion, impofed upon by their
plaufibility, and gained upon by the appearance of truth, was on the point of dif-
charging this faithful Subject, and appoint-
ing another to his poft; but fuddenly recollecting the facred injunction of his father, he immediately applied to the Lionefs, and informing her of the accufations
alledged againft the old Dog, and the fhadow of reafon by which he had been almoft
tempted to remove him, begged her advice
how

how to act : to which he received the
following anfwer : "It is, my fon, mere-
ly the fhadow of reafon indeed ! for no
fubftantial one can they offer for removing
your uncorruptible guard, except to eftablifh themfelves on his deftruction and your
ruin ; but, like many deceitful people,
they have overfhot their mark, and while
they thought they were convincing you of
his worthleffnefs, they were enumerating
thofe virtues which fo particularly render
him deferving the truft repofed in him."

"Be affured he careffes only thofe well
known to be faithful to you ; and if he growls,
it is againft thofe who are rebels in their
hearts, and only want for power to de-
throne you : His barking at night is a
proof of his vigilance and watchfulnefs ;
and his bearing on his body the fcars of
many wounds, redounds greatly to his honor, and fignalizes him for bravery as well
as loyalty, in preferring his duty to you,
to his own life : If he never goes out, he
gives the higheft teftimony of his unfhaken
attachment to you, well knowing he could
not find another to whofe fidelitiy he could,
with fatisfaction to himfelf, truft your facred perfon ; therefore he facrifices every
confideration in devoting himfelf to the
                                    defence

defence of your majefty : And if he makes himfelf heard by his neighbours, he performs a public fervice, giving the alarm on the approach of danger : In fhort, cowardice is not·natural to him, and he ftill poffeffes teeth to execute any deeds his valor fhall diftate, and·to refift any attacks that may be offered him".

. The Lion perfeftly convinced by his mother's reafoning, and rejoicing at having confulted her, declared that during his life, the old dog fhould be his friend,—his guard and companion ; whofe age fhould be crowned with honors, and cherifhed with tendernefs.

M O R A L.

It is not thirft of fame,—it is not a laudable ambition, (however the mean and artful may endeavor, under thofe high-founding expreffions, to veil their dark defigns, for fuch muft be termed the diabolical artifice) that builds a fortune on another man's ruin, undermining his charafter to gratify their own avarice and unfatiable pride : Such have been called, and very properly, the leeches of the ftate.

XXXIX

XXXIX. The Fox, the Wolf, and the Lambs.

There is no nation, however uncivilized; no people, however barbarous, but inherit, from nature, a love of justice, and form a tribunal for the impartial dispensation of it.

FABLE.

ALL the Animals agreed to sit in judgement in turn, hoping that then there would be few opportunities for bribing, and fewer for corruption. About this time the Fox became Judge, when a suit was brought before him, wherein the Wolf was
plaintiff

plaintiff againſt ſome Lambs, whom their
mother, he urged, when dying, had left to
his guardianſhip : but, as her entruſting
them to the care of their natural enemy,
carried in it very little appearance of truth,
the Wolf thought it adviſeable to bribe the
Fox ; promiſing when he was Judge, to
acquit him of all the thefts he committed
in the farmers' yards, and all the murders
he perpetrated on the poultry.

There being only two witneſſes wanting,
but theſe being particularly requiſite, in ſo
bad a cauſe, to give, at leaſt, a colour of
juſtice, he corrupted a Kite and a Vulture,
by promiſing that when the Lambs were
killed, they ſhould have the entrails and
offals. One of the Lambs being interro-
gated, and ordered to give in her defence
againſt two reſpectable witneſſes, ſaid, with
tears in her eyes, that her mother never
would have committed them to the care of
the Wolf, had ſhe had time to make her
will ; but was prevented from any ſuch deciſion by the premature death, the Wolf
had, himſelf, inflicted upon her.

The Wolf firing up, at theſe laſt words,
loudly called for puniſhment and redreſs,
for ſuch a ſcandalous aſperſion of his cha-
racter

raɛter; but the Fox pretending to favor
the Lambs, refuſed to infliɛt any puniſhment, yet at the ſame time, conſigned them
to the care of the Wolf, ſince ſuch was
the laſt decree of their mother.

M O R A L.

A vicious perſon thinks you indebted to
him, if he does not do all the harm he has it
in his power to infliɛt.

XL

XL. The Blind Bear and Bees.

The depravity of human nature is such, that
instances have been known, where profess-
ed friends have refused that relief, which
has afterwards been afforded by an enemy.

F A B L E.

A Bear, unfortunately becoming blind,
occasioned great diſtreſs to his family;
every endeavor was exerted both by his relations and friends to cure him ; and they
were, to appearance, very zealous in ſeek-
ing for medicines, of which they anxiouſ-
ly applied ſeveral, without effect : Great
dependance they placed in the dwarf Al-
der

der, which being particularly recommended, they' made a bath of it, in which they
repeatedly bathed his head ; that alſo failed, and in failing of ſucceſs, diſcovered
the motive which induced them to intereſt
themſelves ſo warmly ; which was, the fear
of the world's condemning them, if they
forſook him, and the little inclination they
had to nurſe and attend him, when he was
no longer able to be of ſervice to them,
but on the contrary, would prove an in-
ſupportable trouble.

Such being their ſentiments, the opinion
of the world ſoon ceaſed to have any
weight, and they entirely forſook him,
with the exception of one or two, not yet
hardened againſt the ſhame of ſuch a conduct ; and who, in the momentary pride of
appearing ſo much more noble-minded
than the others, had ſworn never to quit
him :   Juſt as they had finiſhed profeſſions
which, by appearing in a comparative
view, they thought would enhance their
merits to the world ; a ſwarm of Bees iſſued
from the trunk of a tree, and put to flight
theſe ſincere and faithful friends, who in
their own ſafety, forgot the deplorable and
unprotected ſituation of the poor forſaken
blind Bear.

M   As

As soon as he found himself alone, and perfectly deserted, devoid of every comfort, and every support, labouring under the most dreadful calamity, which disabled him from escaping the attacks of those tormenting tho' diminutive little animals, he raised his eyes to heaven, deploring his miserable condition, and not doubting, but the exquisite pain he felt would soon terminate his life ; whereas, on the contrary, the sting of the Bees, piercing through the film which covered the eye, occasioned an eruption of that body of matter which caused his blindness, and so perfectly cured him, that once more seeing light, he cried out in transport ; "Thanks to the Gods ! who have not only restored me to my bodily sight, but to my mental one also, by discovering the falsity of my friends, and teaching me, according to their command, to respect my enemies ; who may in reality boast of those virtues, which my deceitful friends were indebted to my blind partiality, for appearing to possess."

M O R A L.

To bear affliction with fortitude, reflects honor, and dignifies adversity.

F I N I S.

www.ingramcontent.com/pod-product-compliance
Lightning Source LLC
Chambersburg PA
CBHW020003030726
47500CB00002B/420